HORIZON

DAVID W. ADAMS

CONTENTS

ISBN:
978-1-916582-46-0 [Paperback]
978-1-916582-47-7 [eBook]
978-1-916582-48-4 [Hardcover]

ECHO ON PUBLICATIONS

CONTENT WARNING

The following story contains some, well pretty brutal shit. It's a sci-fi horror. What do you expect. Well, I will tell you what to expect. I'm nice like that. So below are some of the more triggering themes you will find in *Horizon*.

- Graphic descriptions of injury
- Graphic depictions of dead bodies
- Descriptions of mutilation
- Brief mentions of drug dealing
- Body horror
- Claustrophobia/Isolation

If you find any more triggering themes in the book, please let me know and I will update the list accordingly. Your mental health is always the priority, so take breaks where needed. And keep reminding yourself...

...it's just a book, it's just a book...

For Nancy & Richard,

Thank you for always being there to support us when we need it the most.

You've been the shoulder we've needed, and we cannot thank you enough.

PROLOGUE

"Space is nothing but a graveyard. You can fool yourself into thinking it is a magical and wondrous place full of intrigue and exploration, but in reality it was nothing but death and emptiness surrounded in shadows and blood."

These were the words of the founder of *Utopia*. The mission was clear. Earth was dying. Mars was dying. Jupiter was dying. Humanity had done its level best to destroy each and every one of them in the ways you would expect, whilst preaching about climate change prevention measures, and that old adage that the mistakes of the past would not be repeated. But of course they were.

Utopia was designed to seek out new homes for humanity with the ultimate goal of colonisation. The initial vessels were sent out into open space in the year 2332. Seven vessels were dispatched in total, each heading out in a different direction. The founder of this ambitious project was a man by the name of Harry Ransome. He had been a military veteran of four separate interplanetary wars and had been instrumental in bringing about peace with the indigenous species living on the other planets in our solar system.

1

Before they were covertly wiped out, of course.

The fleet led by the *Odyssey*, each held a thousand souls and were due to send monthly reports back to Earth with whatever they had found. Each ship was equipped with an experimental engine which allowed the vessels to travel at multiple times the speed of light. They called it the 'Star Drive' and every human had felt the surge of excitement and possibility the day it was tested for the first time. That first test run was completed by the *Odyssey* and from that moment, that particular vessel became the hero ship for humanity.

The President of Earth herself gave Ransome the highest honour any man could be given. He was given the new rank of Admiral of the Fleet, and given overall command of the mission. The ships of the fleet left the Sol System on 4th December 2332.

The first messages were relayed exactly one month later.

Nothing to report, simply open space and barren moons around desolate planets.

The second messages came one month later, in February.

Same reports.

The third messages never came.

Frantic efforts were made by those on both Earth and the colonies on Mars and Jupiter. Each planet had a starship in reserve should it be needed for an emergency. The Earth ship, *Northwestern*, was dispatched along the known flight path of the *Odyssey*. Again, reports were due monthly. All the while, Earth's resources were dwindling and panic was beginning to set in amongst the population which had now reached twenty-six billion.

The first report came exactly a month later. No signs of Harry Ransome or his ship. Confirmation that their initial report was correct.

The second report came a month later, same as before. Same information, same results.

The third report never came.

Four years passed without anyone hearing or seeing anything from any of the ships. Wars had once again broken out on Earth, with those on Mars and Jupiter attempting to claim sovereignty over the planet by birthright of the first settlers. By the winter of 2340, Earth had been reduced to ash, the population down to less than a billion, and those remaining on Mars and Jupiter had been destroyed. The decision was made by those left alive, to send out an emergency distress call to any species that could hear the humans cry for help.

But what they received back was not what they had expected. They did not receive an answer with promise of help or salvation. They received another distress call.

From Admiral Harry Ransome.

"To anyone in the Sol System, any humans that can hear me. This is Admiral Harry Ransome, on board the Earth vessel Odyssey. We were dispatched by our people almost a decade ago to search for a new home for our people and explore the galaxy. Two months into our journey, we encountered a species called the Darla. They were in a similar state to ourselves, seeking a new home. They told us about a phenomenon they'd become aware of called The Horizon. The Darla gave us a fantastical tale of how this energy nebula would transport you back in time to a place where you were at your happiest.

Naturally, as a military man, I dismissed the notion as having no scientific grounding whatsoever. But my crew began to interact with the Darla, and the more they did so, the more they were convinced The Horizon existed. Fights began breaking out amongst senior officers, and in little to no time, we had our first death on board.

I don't know what possessed me to seek out this place. The Darla appeared to have some kind of telepathic influence over us, and even though I knew it meant we would miss our check in with our monthly transmission to Earth, I ordered us to set course.

Do not come looking for us.

It is too late for us.

Those who left are gone. They entered the Expanse, and they never came back. I heard their screams over the communications channels as if they were inside my own head. Others took the escape pods and launched into the darkness.

There's nothing here.

Space is nothing but a graveyard.

You can fool yourself into thinking it is a magical and wondrous place full of intrigue and exploration, but in reality it was nothing but death and emptiness surrounded in shadows and blood.

We were wrong. I was wrong.

I have only fifty-two crew left on board. I'm turning the Odyssey around and heading for the nearest space station. It's not far from here. Seems to be a traders place of business. Maybe we can barter our way to a nearby home for those of us that are left.

Maybe one day, we will find our way back to you."

That transmission was picked up in 2342.

No further message was ever received.

ONE

2499

"THIS IS THE CAPTAIN! ALL HANDS TO EMERGENCY escape pods!"

The repeating claxon indicating the battle was lost, had been sounding for four minutes and twenty-nine seconds. During that time, eight crew members had lost their lives. Some had turned to sheer panic, and their fight or flight instinct had been scrambled. As another hit struck the hull of the *Belle Vue*, metal beneath the impact twisted and screamed for mercy, before being ripped away with decompression. Darnell Franklin had been next to that bulkhead. As the violent nature of the scene unfolded, his body was torn backwards, impacting with the now jagged edges of the tattered hull, the vacuum of space using it to slice Darnell's body into six uneven pieces. As his blood began to collect in perfectly rounded globules outside of the ship, the emergency forcefield kicked in, numbing the effect of the chaos.

The *Belle Vue* was not a sizeable ship by any means. Designed for a crew of one-hundred-fifty, it was ergonomically designed. No wasted space, no wasted luxuries. And up until twenty seven minutes ago, it had been this crew's home for almost seven years. The narrow corridors wound around the ship's structure like honeycomb, each hallway connecting to another to maximise both accessibility and functionality. Sat at the top of the ship, was the Bridge. And it was the actions in this particular room that had led to what was surely going to be the *Belle Vue's* imminent destruction.

"Roman, there's no response from the escape pods, they're locked in place! I've got crew in there that can't evacuate!"

The panicked voice of the Operations officer, Drusilla Ransome, could barely be heard through the noise of micro explosions, the warning sirens, and the screams of the wounded being helped down towards the medical bay. The Captain, Roman Knight on the other hand, remained resolute, and determined that this ship would not go down at the hands of pirates.

"Hunter! Get down to Deck Three and blow the clamps on the escape pods manually! Get those crewmembers free!"

His first officer, Hunter Dresden, simply nodded at his Captain, and sprinted for the doors at the rear of the bridge, stopping momentarily to glance at Drusilla.

"I'll see you soon sweetheart," he spoke softly to her, before leaving the bridge.

Drusilla felt a tear roll down her cheek, which was exacerbated by the fact a new impact from weapons fire, took out her internal sensors. She could no longer see where anyone was on board. Including Hunter.

"Captain? What are your orders?" shouted weapons officer Noah Sackett. His face sported wide eyes and an expression of pure fear and uncertainty.

Roman leaned in his chair to the left, and ran his opposite

hand across his face. On the viewscreen in front of him, he could see a third vessel approaching. He knew the second they were in range, that would be the end of him, his crew and any hope they had of finding what they had been searching for.

"Weapons status, Noah?"

A few taps into the console later, and Noah gave his answer. It didn't make for encouraging hearing.

"All four disrupter cannons are offline, the power cells have been destroyed. There's no way to fix them. The fore torpedo bay has gone too. I mean that whole fucking section is just... gone... I..."

"Noah!" screamed Roman. "Cut the bullshit and focus for me here. What DO we have?"

Noah closed his eyes and took a deep breath, as yet another shot rocked the ship. The communications station exploded in a shower of shattered glass, fractured wall panels and bundles of severed wiring. The crew member stationed there was blown to pieces.

"We... we have... we have one torpedo left available in the rear bay, but we don't have main engines to turn the ship to use it, and we have three targets!"

Roman cursed their luck. This had been a potential salvage mission, and now half his crew were dead, and pretty soon, the rest would be joining them. He had been warned by so many people he had spoken to that this would be a trap. They had warned him the area was swimming with pirates desperate to strip any ship that wandered into their territory. Resources were scarce across the galaxy, and there was no unity between people anymore.

Think, Roman, think.

An idea came to him in an instant. But it would not be easy. He looked down towards the pilot seat, and although her head was pouring with blood, matting her blonde hair to her shirt, his pilot, Samantha, was still at the controls. She was a tough cookie. Had she not been such an exceptional pilot, Roman would have had her retrained into security.

"Sam, talk to me. What kind of movement do we have?"

"Well boss, we have no star drive, no impulse power and minimal thrusters. We are as close as you can get to a sitting duck!"

Minimal thrusters. That might just do it.

"Dru, can we channel whatever energy we have left into the thrusters? Everywhere except the weapons?"

Drusilla checked her console, and despite the damage, the bypass conduits were still functioning, albeit at minimal power.

"I can do it, but it's gonna surge through the entire system and blow out everything. We'll be lucky to stay in one piece!"

Roman looked around at his crew. Each one nodded in turn. They knew if they didn't try this, then one piece would be a best case scenario.

"Noah, when the ship swings round, I want that torpedo shoved down the lead ship's throat. Understand?"

"Yes Sir!"

"Sam? When the thrusters swing us half way round, I want you to vent the rest of the fuel we have and cut the thrusters. The momentum should carry us round. I want those ships sat in a cloud of flammable shit. Got it?"

Samantha smiled as she realised what he was planning.

"You got it boss."

"Nat.." Roman stopped as he realised his communications officer was now just chunks of seared flesh on the floor next to a completely destroyed communications console. "Does anyone have access to communications?"

"I have internal comms rerouted here," offered Drusilla.

"Open a channel to the crew."

An audible chime echoed around the bridge, and travelled along every corridor still in tact within the ship. Romans deep and gravelly voice boomed throughout the ship.

"All hands, this is the Captain. We are about to try a last ditch attempt to get the ship clear and safe. If this works, we're gonna be propelled fast and hard away from the battle. Forcefields won't work, structural integrity will be compromised, and there's a huge risk that we'll be blown to pieces. But if we don't... those thieving bastards are gonna do that for us anyway. I say we take 'em out with us. Get yourselves to any safe place you can find... and hold on."

Drusilla closed the channel, and Roman gripped the arms of his chair tightly. The third ship was now in range. They were out of time.

"NOW!"

Drusilla fiercely hit her control panel, sending every morsel of power not connected to the weapons surging through a single bypass conduit. As it did so, from the very base of the *Belle Vue*, conduits exploded, walls blew out from their panels, pipes came crashing down from the ceiling and more holes were torn in the side of the ship. The cascading effect lasted mere seconds, but the devastation to the ship was immense. When the power reached the thrusters, they fired into life, indicated on Samantha's panel at five hundred and six percent power. The ship swung violently to starboard, the force of which caused the already buckled ship to creak and groan as if in pain. As the back of the *Belle Vue* reached ninety degrees from its previous position, Samantha cut the power, and initiated a fuel dump. Sparkling vapour cascaded from the rear of the engines, and as the momentum carried the ship round to a full about face, that same momentum threw the fuel into the three advancing ships, which had now taken up an attack posture. The *Belle Vue* was in position.

"FIRE!"

Noah launched the final torpedo, a flash of green briefly lighting up the rear of the ship. The viewscreen switched to an aft view, and Roman slowly climbed to his feet as he watched it soar ever closer to the pirate vessels. Everyone was silent. Their attackers realised too late. The lead ship attempted to turn, but as the torpedo hit the fuel cloud, it ignited around all three ships. The lead ship's nose ignited with such force, it blew it away from the rest of the vessel, sparking multiple explosions throughout the ship. Three seconds later and it blew apart entirely. The close proximity to the other two ships caught them in its wake, and they too were consumed by fire.

Momentary elation ran through Roman's body, before he saw the shockwave of what had just happened flying towards them at break neck speed.

"EVERYBODY HANG ON!" he screamed.

The shockwave hit the *Belle Vue* so hard, it tore both engines from the side of the ship, drifting away in random directions until they were nowhere to be seen. The remaining mass of the ship burst forward, rolling over and over in the wake of the wave, bulkheads crumbling, fire tearing through sections of the corridors vaporising anyone in its way. On the escape pod level, Hunter was clinging on to one of the support beams for dear life as the artificial gravity failed. He had managed to free three escape pods, but two had been struck by the severed engines and destroyed and the third was caught in the initial blast.

"BRIDGE! COME IN! CAN YOU HEAR ME?"

But internal comms were now a thing of the past. All systems were effectively destroyed as they barrel rolled towards oblivion. On the bridge, Roman was pinned in his seat, thankful for the foresight to install a harness after a previous encounter. Drusilla was unconscious against the legs of her console, pinned to the floor by a nineteen inch piece of metal skewering her leg to the deck beneath. Noah was gripping a bundle of wires from underneath his now destroyed console with everything he had left, and Samantha was doing the same.

As the shockwave dissipated, the ship stopped rolling, but their momentum didn't. As the viewscreen flickered back into life, Roman was able to see a planet coming up fast. There was no way they could break free in time. He looked around the room at his crew, his friends. This was all his fault. He had led them into this, and now he was going to get them killed after all. As he tried to stand, a deafening screech echoed around them, and the ship shook violently to the side, sending Roman back down into his chair. As he watched, the entire rear half of the *Belle Vue* flew past them on an altered trajectory, spilling crew members into space. As Roman looked on, he saw Hunter's lifeless body drift away from the wreckage, and moments later, it was incinerated as it entered the planet's atmosphere.

This was it.

The *Belle Vue* was going down with all hands.

And her Captain.

TWO

Yesterday's Humans. Hardly a terrible insult, but enough of one to cut right through whatever patience Roman had left. It was a term he had heard before that was meant to indicate them as an extinct species. Of course while that was not yet proven, it was highly likely. But this visitor had chosen the wrong day to screw with Roman Knight.

The first bone to crunch on his opponent's face was his left eye socket. Roman had never managed to burst an eyeball before, but the sound and vibrational sensation in his fist was oddly satisfying. None of the other patrons in the trading station dared approach the human.

Roman Knight was a vastly imposing figure. He stood six-foot-five, broad and tensed shoulders, an impenetrably dark-haired close cut beard, and black straight hair that hung past his shoulders. If his appearance and the cold gaze of his grey eyes wasn't enough to ward off those who dared approach him, the sleeve of tattoos running down both arms surely would. The left displayed tribal markings from his ancestral

15

home of Samoa on Earth, whilst the right was a mural of those he had lost within his family. A tattoo which was recently updated to include his former first officer.

As the jaw of the offending alien cracked, and he lost consciousness, Roman lifted his now limp body into the air, and slammed it down through the nearest table, splintering the metal with such force, several shards sheared off and embedded in Roman's shins. He didn't seem to notice, despite the audible gasps of those around him.

"He's paying my tab," Roman spoke to the vendor with a dark and gravelly timbre whilst giving him a hardened stare.

"Y... yes... yes that's what I believe he said too."

Roman leaned over the counter, collected his engine parts, and walked out through the automatic doors at the front of the store.

Today had not been a good one for Roman Knight. Then again, was there ever a good day to bury a friend? The sheer guilt of the situation was now weighing down every muscle in Roman's body and the blame was almost too much to bear. Unnecessary risks, and all in the name of chasing ghosts. Now he was once again without a ship, and he and his crew were stranded having lost their doctor. He knew they still believed in him, even if he didn't, but he stood outside their rented accommodation, not wanting to go inside. The memory of the morning's service was replaying over and over again, and the rage within began to grow, Roman's eyes flicking left to right faster and faster, his teeth gritting, muscles tensing, until finally he let out a roar of rage and launched the engine parts through the ground floor window, glass shattering everywhere as he took deep breaths to try and calm himself.

"Thanks for that. I really wanted coils in my cereal bowl. Was tired of cornflakes anyway."

The soothing voice immediately brought calm to Roman's

mind, and he even managed a small smile in the corner of his mouth as the source of the joke walked out the metal front door, holding an engine coil dripping with milk.

Drusilla Ransome was usually the only person who could get through to Roman. Of course the others believed it was her telepathic abilities which allowed her to do so, but she knew otherwise. Drusilla had been seeing Hunter, the first officer of the *Belle Vue* before his death three years ago. But for the last twelve months, her and Roman had become closer.

She was stunningly beautiful and some of the others had been jealous of Hunter when he managed to secure a first date with her. Drusilla was five-feet-nine, had well defined muscles of her own, and was immediately recognisable by her deep blue hair which trailed down her back. Being only half human made her the odd one out, but the hair was the only noticeable physical aspect of her unknown lineage to outsiders.

Now of course, Caleb was dead and the tension was palpable, bringing all of those painful memories of their arrival here rushing back to the surface.

"Shouldn't leave your breakfast near a broken window then."

They spent several moments staring into each other's eyes, before Drusilla cleared her throat and gestured for them to go inside.

"There's something you need to see. Noah thinks you were right."

Roman's eyes widened slightly and he followed her inside, only noticing a few seconds later, that they were holding hands, which he quickly let go of before they entered the living room.

"Roman, you were onto something!" exclaimed Noah, who regretted his level of outburst and excitement when he recalled the events of the morning. "Sorry, I didn't mean to be disrespectful."

Roman held up his hand and shook his head.

"Don't worry about it. If you've found something, maybe Caleb's death won't have been for nothing."

Noah seemed reinvigorated by his Captain's blessing, and regained his excitement, tapping into a mobile tablet before grabbing a holographic image and launching it into the air, where it expanded for all to see, bathing the room in an eerie green glow.

"I found her."

Noah said nothing more, and simply let the others absorb what they were looking at. The image itself was more of a simulation of an asteroid field, and the longer they stared at it, the further into the belt the image moved, until it settled on an incredibly large asteroid which appeared to have a cavern on the western side. The hologram then began generating text, and a flashing beacon appeared in the centre of the cavern, and the text formed a label pointing at said beacon.

"No fucking way," Drusilla blurted out.

"Yes fucking way," came Noah's reply.

Roman's eyes were burning with desire at the image before him, and Drusilla could feel those emotions run through her, being in such close proximity. The effect caused her to smile. Roman glared at the location marker, and then at the label hovering over the asteroid. Wanting to ensure everyone was aware of the significance of the find, he read the label aloud.

"Location confirmed... *USS Odyssey.*"

THREE

SAT ON HIS BED, STARING OUT THE WINDOW, ROMAN could see the burnt and fractured hull of his ship the *Belle Vue*, and the rest of the engineers led by Noah, working on fitting the new engine coils in the hope that she might fly again. They had been on this colony world for almost three years, ever since they crash landed in the Northern Hemisphere. The impact had killed the majority of those left behind, but after discovering a traders settlement two months later, the task of essentially rebuilding the *Belle Vue* got under way. Moving the wreckage to the south of the planet had been expensive, but the events of the battle with the pirates had hardened Roman, and many people on the outpost were now afraid of him. Because of that fear, discounted parts and favours had meant that engines were the last thing to be rebuilt on his ship. There was no guarantee she would fly again, but in truth, Roman didn't care if she flew for long and then burned up, as long as it was enough time to get them to the *Odyssey*.

He had dreamt about that ship his entire life. Being a human born out in the cosmos gave him and the others like him a yearning. For knowledge, for a connection to their heritage, but most of all, to give them some kind of anchor of where they truly came from. It had been one-hundred-sixty years since the final transmission from Harry Ransome. Just five years later, Earth was nothing but an empty and dusty wasteland. Roman never knew his parents. All he knew about them was that they were the children of the crew members from a ship called *Northwestern*, which was found spread over an ocean moon. He, Noah and Hunter were found together with a data pad containing their names, parental details, and medical data by an exploration vessel taking scans of the moon's indigenous whale species. They had been handed over to an intergalactic orphanage six months later, where they spent the rest of their childhood.

That was until yet another cosmic war played out and the orphanage was destroyed in what was described as collateral damage by the invading military. Roman, Noah and Hunter escaped the carnage and made it onto an evacuation ship. They were all just fourteen years old. Ever since then, they had spent their lives hopping from one planet to another, one space station to another, all the while watching as one by one, species vanished, wars played out, and death came for everyone. The only hope they had was finding the *Odyssey*. In the century which followed Admiral Ransome's final message, all of the Earth ships had been found either in pieces, crashed beyond repair, or in the case of the *Destiny*, completely vapourised, crew and all, caught in the ice trail of a comet.

Except for the *Odyssey*.

That was the only ship known to have survived long enough to head for safe harbour. Whether they made it there was another question. But no wreckage had ever been found. And with the arrival of Drusilla Ransome, seemingly descended from the Admiral himself, the fires of desperation were fuelled even further. Sadly, it was that fuel which cost so many lives that day, and now the life of his doctor.

Roman winced as he pulled another shard of splintered metal from his leg. It was only when he decided to head up to shower that he had even noticed the specks of blood on his cargo trousers. The damage had been more severe than it appeared, leading him to stitch up three lacerations. With no doctor in the crew following Caleb's death, Roman thought there would be many more instances where he may have to patch himself up yet. Or worse, others in his crew.

The *Belle Vue* now had a crew of seventeen. The core of that crew were Roman, Drusilla and Noah. There was then the engineering detail of Avery, Samson, Carlos, Tatyana and Lucille who had been children of the *Mauritania*. Maintenance were different to engineering. They lacked the skillset of replacing or installing new parts, and instead patched things up, cleaned the ship, and were generally younger with lesser experience. There were also five members of that particular department. That left the chef, Alonso, weapons officer Matteo, new communications officer Aliah and now science officer Samantha. Without a ship to fly, there had not been much call for a pilot, and with Roman terrifying everyone there, there had been no need for much security either.

With such a small crew, most of them doubled up in duties. Noah often lent a hand to Samantha in science and research, while Drusilla tended to lead any potentially dangerous missions as tactical chief. Caleb had started to train Roman in medical procedures when he'd been killed just twenty-four hours prior in a botched expedition to discover a potential source of fuel for the new engines. A cave in had been triggered and Caleb had been crushed to death.

Roman tried to push that to the back of his mind. The last

shard of metal clinked into a small bowl placed next to him on the khaki bed spread, and he gingerly stood, lifted the bowl and placed it on the side next to the mirror. The bathroom was almost the size of the bedroom, and each person had their own facilities. Although the core crew were friendly with each other, the other departments tended to like their own space, and so when they performed their emergency landing on *Azanti Prime*, Roman made sure they found suitable accommodation for the foreseeable future.

He waved his hand across the sensor and the shower surged into life, the water instantly scolding hot. Perfect. Maybe Roman could burn the dread and sadness away and gain some kind of feeling back again. He lifted his shirt over his head and launched it back into the bedroom, the doorway already obscured by the steam rising from the water's immense heat. Roman climbed into the shower, and stood directly under the falling water. His hair clung to his shoulders which sported several scars of their own.

The left shoulder bore the aftermath of a seven inch blade plunged into Roman's back when he tried to negotiate with bounty hunters who had been set on him after a trade deal gone wrong. The right shoulder was home to a circular wound, glowing white against the rest of his caramel skin, with vein-like splinters spreading out from the centre. A point blank shot with an energy rifle was the result of pirates attempting to kidnap Drusilla five months earlier. He had stepped into the path of the weapon discharge to protect Noah and took the full force. They weren't sure he would survive. But Roman's composure had been resolute. He would find the *Odyssey* or die trying. There was no in between.

After twenty minutes of standing under the hot water, Roman began to feel as though he was beginning to overheat internally, and moved to wave his hand across the sensor to turn the water off. However, another hand caught his, and pulled it away.

Roman looked up in the direction of Drusilla, who was now standing at his side, her piercing blue eyes staring back at him. She gripped his hand tightly for a moment before letting go and stepping back. Roman watched as she raised her shirt over her head and let it drop to the floor. His eyes never left hers, despite what she was doing. Once she was fully undressed, she moved forwards and stepped into the shower alongside Roman. Her vibrant blue hair instantly matted to her chest, shoulders and neck, and she raised her hands to rest on the back of Roman's head.

She felt him ease in her hands, like the tension had begun to melt away. They both knew the timing was terrible, with Caleb laid to rest only hours before, but they also knew they had needed each other. Beyond the last few days, but for the last couple of years. Stolen moments of companionship, sitting in empty half repaired corridors, simply being with one another staring out of a window at the stars. Never crossing the line of 'more than friends', but always testing their will power and the boundaries of their relationship.

But this was different. Times were different. And the barriers were now gone.

As Drusilla's lips crushed against Roman's, the two of them embraced each other tightly. The kisses became more passionate, the water from the rain head of the shower cascading over both of them, scalding their skin as it did so. Roman's hands moved over Drusilla's body with comfort and gentleness, and she reciprocated gripping his buttocks, squeezing gently. Roman moved away for a moment, and brushed the droplets of water away from her cheeks, and cupped her chin in his hand. This was it. There was no going back now.

Drusilla moved his hand away, planted her lips on his once more, and raised herself onto Roman's hips. As the two of them moved together finally able to love each other as they had fantasised about for so long, the entire top floor of the house became consumed in the steam from the shower. All thoughts of the *Odyssey* were pushed away and in the moment there was only Roman and Drusilla.

Perhaps making love in the shower was where they should have stayed. Because unknown to them, the *Odyssey* was never going to be the salvation they had hoped for.

FOUR

FOR A SUPPOSEDLY EXTINCT SPECIES, THE DARLA WERE considerably more active in the quadrant as one might expect. They, like many others had been near wiped out over the last hundred years, but this particular group weren't like the others at all.

The Darla race were a telepathic species, humanoid in appearance, but with small ridges on the bridge of their nose, and similar markings in a vertical pattern across their cheeks. They were able to influence the thoughts and feelings of those in their immediate vicinity. Unfortunately, this gift also made them vulnerable to similar intrusions from other species with similar abilities.

This had led them to the Expanse.

Darven did not remember the journey to this place, nor the instance in which he began it. From his point of view, he had just gotten here, and was as equally surprised and confused as the rest of his small crew. As their scout ship slowed to a stop, the stars vanished from view entirely, leaving a black and empty void ahead of them. The Expanse had been documented as existing by very few ships, most of which were long gone. But the Darla were veterans of this place. They were often called to this place by someone... or something.

Darven and his crew believed this was their first time at the boundary of the Expanse, but of course they were entirely wrong. This group of Darla had been here not once before, or twice, but a grand total of sixty-four times. And each time they had returned with their hallways showered in blood and hounded by screams as those they carried were torn apart.

The Darla were incredibly long lived, and Darven himself was over two hundred years old. Though he didn't remember it, his first visit to the Expanse was onboard a human vessel. *Odyssey* had brought him here, or more correctly, he had brought the *Odyssey* here. It was one of the rare occasions that anyone besides the Darla had *left* the border of this place. A record those dwelling within the Expanse had not forgotten.

A being of such hunger and ravenous appetite, the dwindling nature of the galaxy's inhabitants was beginning to drive them insane. No food, no existence.

It was at this point that Darven felt his consciousness pushed to the side once again, and a voice boomed within him. It felt as though a group of vines had entered his body and were snaking their way around his insides, taking over the controls of his movements.

"You will bring them to us."

Darven's face was static, but inside his mind, he was screaming to be let out of the cage he had been placed in within his own body. The pain would be temporary for him. Once he and his crew completed their mission, his mind would be erased, and the process would start again.

"You WILL bring them to US!"

Darven's hands moved across the navigational controls, and the ship slowly edged into the darkness of the Expanse, much to the confusion of his crew, who were not yet under their usual spell, as their Captain was.

"Darven?" asked one of the female Darla. "What are you doing?"

Darven, of course, said nothing. He couldn't. Once the ship was fully emersed in the nothingness, he cut the engines, and lowered the ship's shields.

"Darven?" she asked again.

The lights went out across the ship, plunging them into darkness. The two females and other male colleague began fumbling around looking for a way to power the systems back online.

"What's he doing?"

"I've no idea! He cut main power, and I can't get it back online!"

A loud clunk echoed around them as the backup lights kicked in, and everyone was bathed in a red glow. Darven stood directly in front of them all, and as they began backing away from him, one of them reaching for a weapon, Darven spoke.

Except it wasn't Darven's voice.

"We... must... *feed...*"

The terror gripped the others immediately, and the male lifted his pistol upwards, but as he moved to fire at Darven, an all encompassing black shadow darted across in front of him with such speed, it left a gust of wind in its wake. The weapon clattered to the floor, and a brief cry of pain was heard, before the sound of gargling, and then silence.

Drip. Drip. Drip.

"Wh- what the hell was that?"

Swinging her head around, one of the female colleagues followed the sound, before her foot slipped in something slick. Her left leg gave way beneath her, and her ankle twisted to the right, the snap clearly audible. As she lay on the ground screaming, she lifted her hand to her face and as the red light illuminated it, she saw her hand was caked in blood. *Warm* blood.

Slowly raising her gaze to the ceiling above her, she saw the mangled body of her male colleague hanging above her, his blood dripping onto the ground below where she had fallen.

Darven's body remained rigid and still as the shadows tore through the ship, the sounds of the crew screaming echoing down the metal hallways.

And then... silence.

FIVE

"AFT TORPEDOES?"

"Nope."

"Fore torpedoes?"

"Nope."

"Disruptors?"

"Nope. We do have a full stock of food though."

Roman was growing increasingly frustrated at the negative responses that Noah was giving to his checklist. He was already consumed by guilt about the time he had spent the previous day with Drusilla. He did not need to hear that his ship may not only fail to take off, but that should they need to, they couldn't even defend themselves.

"So what are we supposed to do if pirates come for us again? Throw a fucking watermelon at them? Somehow I doubt getting a seed stuck in their teeth would be a big enough distraction to stop trying to kill us!"

Roman threw his pad against the wall where it shattered and fell to the ground. He had not slept for almost forty-eight hours. Finally getting together with Drusilla had not provided the relief he had hoped. The guilt of betraying his former first officer was now even heavier on his shoulders. The fact Hunter had been dead for three years meant nothing. His temper was shorter, and as a result, several previously repaired sections of the *Belle Vue* had needed more repairs after colliding with Roman's fists.

"Listen Roman, you wanted to launch ASAP. We just haven't had time to finish the installation of the weapons. The engines are set, or at least as set as they can be. We have food and water, we have medical supplies, and all of our scanning equipment and sensors are fully functional. Given a little more time, we could have her ready for a fight."

Roman turned to his friend.

"How much time?"

"Tuesday."

Roman laughed out loud for the first time in what felt like eons, and Noah joined him. It felt good, and like everything was good with their lives again. But it lasted only a moment. He slumped down onto a nearby supply crate, and swept his hand through his hair, pushing it back over his shoulders.

"Look, Roman. I know you want everything in pristine working order. But you know as well as I do why you wanna get up there so fast. If we found the signature of the *Odyssey*, then someone else probably has too. I can install minimal weapons en route, but as defenceless as we may be right now, I think you're doing the right thing in getting us up there quickly."

And there it was again.

Unwavering allegiance from the crew that he continued to get killed. He had no idea what he had done to earn such unwavering loyalty, but right now he could not have been more grateful for it. He reached across and patted his friend on the shoulder, and got up to walk out of the cargo bay.

"Oh and Roman?" called Noah.

"Yeah?"

"There's a blue hair stuck to your beard."

Noah gave Roman a wink, and a wry smile, before carrying on cataloguing the cargo. Roman smiled to himself, trying to disguise the mild panic at being found out so quickly. But then he relaxed. He knew Noah would keep his mouth shut. Next to Hunter, Noah was Roman's best friend, having grown up together.

Outside in the corridor, Roman hit a communications panel on the wall, and leaned to speak into it.

"Sam, you ready to go?"

A brief moment of static, before Samantha's voice came through loud and clear.

"All ready to go boss. Landing gear is fully operational, and engines have checked out. Pretty sure I remember which buttons to push. More or less."

A smile returned to Roman's face.

"Just waiting on your presence on the bridge."

"I'm on my way."

Drusilla couldn't quite figure out how, but the take-off from the planet surface had been even smoother than before the crash. There had been barely a ripple, even as they rose through the clouds at speed and broke through the atmosphere, leaving Azanti Prime far below. However, the smooth ride wasn't her main focus. No, that sat in the second hand Captain's chair in the centre of the bridge. A figure of uncertainty plunging into the darkness searching for some kind of proverbial goldmine. Roman's obsession may not have been as wild and crazy-eyed as most men determined to get what they want, but it was there. Lying beneath the skin, tearing at his flesh from the inside, driving him day and night to find some kind of belonging.

She too had strong reason to find the *Odyssey*. She carried the name of Ransome, but was not fully human. Her ancestry was hidden from her. She suspected a descendant of Harry Ransome was the human side of her, hence the name. But as for the other side? The side of her that naturally sported stark blue hair, gave her enhanced strength and the ability to project telepathically was of unknown origin. The only way she had known her name was Ransome was due to the details found on her as a baby. Like Roman and the others, she had been an orphan. But she was found by a ship comprised entirely of androids. They were the creation of a scientist from the Andromeda Galaxy, of which very few people had entered. Naturally, the scientist had perished and the androids continued as programmed. Exploring new worlds, and collecting data.

Not many people had crossed the boundaries between galaxies for one reason. Expense. With fewer and fewer surviving species and resources vanishing from the cosmos, fuel was expensive. In order to cross galaxies, not only would you need some kind of stasis system on board which in itself was of incredible monetary value, but you'd need more fuel than you could actually carry.

This at least narrowed down Drusilla's origins most likely to this galaxy. She just didn't know where. Perhaps there were answers on board the *Odyssey* for her too. But after the encounter with Roman, she had begun to feel more disconnected to him than before. The moment was enjoyable, intense and the climax to a long and drawn out desire to be together. However, the aftermath felt hollow, empty, and somehow just wrong. She was still drawn to him, but the desire was being overwhelmed by confusion and uncertainty.

Fortunately, they now had bigger fish to fry.

"How's the star drive looking, Sam?"

"Noah's got that thing glowing like the brightest star, and ready to punch it, on your command."

Noah couldn't help but grin widely next to her. While he never looked for open praise, he also never failed to enjoy it as publicly as possible.

"Let's save the grinning contest until we come out the other side in one piece, huh?"

Noah's smile vanished, giving Roman the slightest tinge of satisfaction. He looked around at everybody, and took a deep breath before talking to them all.

"This is it. We are about to make the biggest find in our history. I know we aren't some kind of military ship, and I know we don't hold ranks, or stick to a certain set of regulations. But I've come to love and respect each and every one of you. I just wanted you to know that before we do this. Are we ready?"

The speech caught Drusilla completely off guard. She had never seen Roman this tender towards the entire crew before, at least the entire bridge crew. She also did not fail to notice the way he stared intently at her as he said the words 'love and respect.'

Sam and Noah declared they were ready, and instinctively, everyone sat upright in their chairs, grabbed hold of the handles on the sides, and tensed their bodies in readiness. With a deep breath exhaled through his nose, Roman gripped the arms of his own chair, and nodded as he said the words.

"Punch it."

SIX

"ALERT! CONDITION RED! ALERT!"

Smoke filled the bridge, panels once again popping off from their various mountings. The sirens replaced by vocal confirmation that they were indeed once again in an insurmountable period of trouble. A small fire had broken out in a conduit directly beneath the doors to the bridge, cutting off their exit, and both Noah and Sam had been thrown from their seats onto the hard floor, sustaining minor injuries in the process.

"REPORT!" Roman yelled over the sound of the computer warning, to anyone who could answer him.

"Fucking coils!" yelled Noah as he climbed back up to his seat. "They've fractured! We're leaking coolant into space, and I've lost all altitude control!"

Sam echoed her colleague's distress with even more worrying news.

"Helm controls are offline! I've got no power over a goddamn thing here Captain!"

Drusilla was next to add her urgency into the mix.

"Roman, we've got fractures all along the hull all

throughout the ship. The stress the engines are putting on our integrity is gonna tear the ship apart!"

Glowing like the brightest star, eh? Roman glared at Noah, but in truth, he should have known buying stolen or pirated engine parts came with a risk, especially given the inactivity of the *Belle Vue*. Once again, he had endangered his ship and crew, and this time, there may be no saving it.

"How far are we away from the asteroid field?" he asked, as he clambered towards Sam.

"Half a lightyear away, but I'm not sure we'll make it that far."

Roman looked at Noah, who simply nodded in agreement.

"The coils are fried, but the engines are still drawing power and trying to engage. With no helm control, we can't turn them off. Simply put, boss, the ship is gonna fly itself apart."

Panic gripped Roman's chest and he frantically charged over to Drusilla's station, putting one hand on the back of her chair, and gesturing with the other one.

"Would it be possible, to teleport us onto the *Odyssey* if we were in range?"

Drusilla looked at him like he had gone insane.

"You cannot be fucking serious Roman! Do you know how dangerous that is?"

"I know exactly how dangerous it is, Dru. That's why I'm asking if it can be done!"

"We're not on a stable course, it's hardly a straight line we're travelling in! We'd have to be within one-hundred-thousand metres to guarantee a destination, and by that point, the bridge might be all that's left!"

Roman's eyes flicked back and forth as his mind whizzed trying to come up with some kind of plan. Drusilla was right.

They had to be within a thousand metres, or they risk being rematerialized in outer space, or worse, not at all. She was also right about the bridge being all that was left. It was designed to operate as a lifeboat if needed, and so had docking clamps integrated beneath it, and a triple thickness of hull. He had made his decision.

"All hands, this is the Captain. Drop whatever you're doing, and make your way to the bridge immediately. You have two minutes. Roman out."

Noah, Sam, and Drusilla all looked at him.

"The engines are mounted either side at the rear of the ship. They're pushing us to the point of disintegration. So what's the most logical thing to do? Get the fuck away from the engines."

Noah caught on to his boss' plan, and staggered to one of the rear wall panels, ripping it from its mount, and revealing a damaged, but still functional fire extinguisher. Roman did the same on the opposite side, and together, they targeted the fire, subduing it enough for the rest of the crew to run across. When the last member of maintenance was in, they threw the extinguishers through the doors, and as the fire reared up again, they flipped the emergency bulkhead and sealed it out.

"ALERT! CONDITION RED! ALERT!"

"Someone shut that fucking thing off!" Roman screamed, and Drusilla kindly obliged.

"Four thousand metres, Roman," Sam spoke with a definitive tremble in her voice. "The rear of the ship is breaking up!"

"Blow us clear, Noah!" he replied.

"Aye!"

Five loud bangs could be heard, and small columns of smoke burst out from under the deck panels surrounding the room. The entire bridge itself shifted to the right as the force of the small detonations pushed them clear of the rest of the ship. They were still hurtling towards the asteroid belt at breakneck speed, but they were in one piece. As the ship veered round beneath them, it overtook them, the engines glowing brighter than the crew's eyes could take. One engine exploded, sending the rest of the ship spiralling even faster. The rear of the vessel smashed into the side of a medium sized asteroid, and in seconds, the rest of the structure was dashed on the rocks, the second engine erupting on impact.

The *Belle Vue* was gone.

Attention then turned back to the danger the crew were still very much in.

"Two thousand metres!" shouted Drusilla.

"Everybody stand perfectly still! This is gonna be tight!"

Everybody huddled around their consoles, and those who were without a seat, simply braced themselves against the wall.

"Fifteen hundred metres!"

Roman closed his eyes tightly.

"One thousand metres! I've got a lock!"

Noah looked up at the viewscreen, and the impending doom of the asteroid absorbing his entire vision.

"Oh shit."

"Hang on!"

There was a bright flash as dozens of green streaks of light flew down from the ceiling, each encapsulating a member of the crew. It wrapped around them like a forcefield, and with a singular pulse, the person within each was seemingly vapourised, before the beams shot through the floor. The bridge was empty when it collided with the face of the asteroid, but the explosion was immense. There was nothing left of it when the fires dimmed out, and a large crack formed on the asteroid itself.

The crack stopped as it crossed one side of the rock, and a fragment broke free exposing a new but jagged surface to open space. The chunk that drifted away bounced off several others as it moved out of the belt, and was lost in the shadow of a large approaching vessel. Pointed in design, with a large glass window at the fore, lights from control panels lit up the face of the pilot.

As he gazed upon the tiny pieces of wreckage from the *Belle Vue*, Darven smiled intently.

SEVEN

THE SMELL HIT NOAH FIRST. NOT THE FLICKERING lights, or the humming in his head from the less than gentle impact... *but the smell*.

His hands grasped at the floor, but could find no traction, and before long, he felt his entire body sliding to the left. Sticking out a leg, he managed to anchor his foot against a piece of wall trim to stop his decline. Shaking his head, and pulling his shirt up to cover his nose and mouth, he looked up. For a moment, he thought he saw something, but as his head was swimming, he dismissed it as an effect of the teleportation. As his vision focussed and he was able to take a look around him, he could see he was indeed crouched against a wall onboard an old Earth ship. The floor was shiny as the day it had been commissioned, he wagered, and was a dark grey surface, bordered by thick white lines of the same material. The lights above were in two uniform lines running the length of the corridor, either side of a similar grey colour to the floor, but this time in carpeted material.

The ship appeared to be at a forty-five degree angle, but despite the age of the vessel, the artificial gravity was still functioning. In fact, only the light panel directly above Noah was flickering. The rest were fully lit and steady.

But that *smell*.

Where was it coming from? Noah planted both feet on the floor, and using the trim his foot had been against, he pushed himself forward, climbing slowly up the inclined deck, the smell getting stronger as he went. His nose, albeit burning from the stench of decay, led him around a sweeping corner, where he passed several computer panels, on standby, and to a door which was slightly ajar. On the other side, was darkness, but there was no doubt this was the source of the acrid fumes.

There was a name plate on the door in question.

Commander Sayid Chowdry, Crew Quarters, Room 47AT.

Noah had an increasingly bad feeling about this. Nevertheless, he was currently alone on a ship that if it was indeed their target, was over one-hundred and fifty years old. He placed one hand on each of the doors, and prised it open. As he did so, a figure lunged forward at him, sending him flying backwards. But he had not escaped this figure, he had become intwined with it. As he rolled down the corridor back the way he had come, with each roll, more and more of the rotting flesh from Chowdry's corpse forced its way onto Noah's body, falling from the bones as if it had been cooked. Bodily fluids soaked into Noah's clothes, and he screamed as his arm went through Chowdry's ribcage and out the other side, unable to get free.

The rolling came to an abrupt stop as the mass of Chowdry and Noah impacted against a cargo bay door with such force that Chowdry's head came loose and landed in his lap. Noah was still screaming so loud that he couldn't hear the voices of Sam and Roman standing beside him, trying to calm him down.

"Noah! It's okay! It's just a body!"

After a few moments, Sam simply leaned forward and slapped Noah across the face, silencing him at once. Roman looked at her accusingly.

"What? He needed to snap out of it!"

Roman shook his head, and leaned forward, with Sam's help prising their friend from the entangled situation he had found himself in. Noah took several short, sharp breaths, before switching to longer, deeper ones, and eventually, calmed himself down again.

"There were three more just like him back there," Sam explained, pointing to another two sets of crew quarter doors which were now closed. "Looks like they died here after impact."

The logic was there as far as the reason bodies would be here, but for Noah, it didn't add up as to why they were in this state of decomposition. His mind now clearing, he had to ask himself the question. A question he chose to voice to his Captain.

"Are we alone here?"

Roman and Sam looked confused, and the pilot responded first.

"Noah, it's just us here. The crew look to be scattered around, but we're the only lifesigns."

Noah closed his eyes tightly as he articulated his words as best as he could.

"Then why do we have freshly decomposing crew members falling out of their quarters instead of skeletons, or perfectly preserved bodies?"

Roman's heart rate shot up. Shit. Noah was right. If the doors had been open this whole time, they'd be looking at skeletons. The environmental systems were working, there were no power shortages and no hull breaches, remarkably. That meant the bodies would have decomposed naturally. Even if the doors had been sealed, the same conditions would have existed in the crew quarters as outside, so the same scenario should have played out. But these bodies could only realistically have been a week old. Two at most.

"So that means..." Sam began.

"That means," interrupted Roman, "that these bodies aren't the crew."

"Which also means," started Noah, "that we aren't alone here after all."

EIGHT

DRUSILLA WAS THE ONLY PERSON TO MATERIALISE ON the bridge. And immediately, she wished she hadn't. The artificial gravity on the bridge was not functioning, and a nearby control panel alerted her as she floated past, that all bridge resources had been diverted to the rest of the ship. The design was sleek and simple. The room was semi-circular in design, with a curve at the rear of the room, and a straight edge near what she assumed was the viewscreen, but in actuality was a wall-sized window. The floors were smooth and constructed of a hard, marble-like material in a deep red hue, bordered all around the room with thick white stripes of the same construction. The furnishings in contrast were white. Both the Captain and First Officer's chairs sat in the middle, in a slightly elevated position and were made of a leather-like material. The same was true of the bases and trims of the work stations, of which there was one continual bank of black glass wrapping the entire back wall, curving half way round each side, with just the gap in the middle for the rear doors.

All of this proved problematic for a floating Drusilla, who

had no surface to grab onto. She was several feet above the chairs, and the walls were smooth with little to no texture. Eventually, she turned herself upside down, and waited for her momentum to carry her up to one of the walls. She then attempted to climb down the wall like a spider, until she reached the floor, and used as little energy as she could to crawl to the chair at the nearest station.

She positioned herself in the chair, and then took off her belt, wrapping it around the back of the chair, and looping it through two buckles on her jacket, thereby keeping her in place. It was then that she looked at the computer panel and discovered the confirmation of their intended destination. Printed in the top right corner of the glass screen was a label.

Panel 24-J, Main Bridge, USS Odyssey.

The station was fully functional, and Drusilla was desperate to dive straight into the crew manifest and extract all the records she could to try and pin down her ancestry.

But she didn't have to.

The console was locked into one mode. It was the communications station, and on the screen was a flashing message.

Message awaiting playback.

Rather tentatively, Drusilla reached forward and tapped the 'command' button, and the screen sparked into life. She leapt back at the sight of a man appearing on the screen before her. His face was weathered, his eyes sunken and surrounded by deep and dark lines. White stubble covered the lower half of his face, the corner by his mouth sporting a streak of dried blood. But it was his eyes that chilled Drusilla to the bone. They were cobalt blue.

Like her eyes.

The message began to play automatically, and Drusilla

felt her nails digging into her thighs as her entire body tensed up.

'This... this is the final entry to my log. Should it be found, then my attempt to bury the Odyssey will have been successful. The auto-destruct sequence is set to abort upon successful impact at the targeted location.

My name is Admiral Harry Ransome. I was the founder of the Utopia project, designed from the ground up to save humanity and help spread our wings amongst the stars. By now I am sure you will be aware that our mission failed. We did not find salvation among the stars. We did not find peace or comfort in the arms of other species. We found only darkness, deceit and blood.

I am recording this message on April 5th 2345. It has been two years since I sent my last transmission to Earth. I hope it reached them. My crew and I were targeted by a telepathic race known as the Darla. Appearing friendly at first, they soon used their abilities to convince my crew to go in search of a phenomenon called the Horizon. It is some kind of spatial distortion, which they claimed would transport a person backward in time to a moment where they were at their happiest.

Fucking bullshit mind tricks.

Some of these officers were so stupid, and so naïve. Fucking weaklings! They broke almost immediately. Took our escape pods and fucked off into the darkness without orders. I confronted their leader, but he assured me the place was real, and it was open to scientific examination upon our arrival. I said no, and threw those bastards off my ship. Half of those who were left went with them, but I kept my mind strong.

At least I thought I had.

I don't know if it was the telepathic link, but I knew they

were dead when I felt their pain that night, and heard the Darla screaming inside my own mind.

I sent my message to Earth, and headed for the last trading station we had passed about two months prior. We landed, gathered supplies, and made enquiries about potential lodging there. The people of Azanti Prime were friendly enough, although half of them seemed to be pirates or thieves. At this point we weren't operating by regulations anymore, so I thought fuck it.

That's when the nightmares started.

Two days later, I woke in a cold sweat after having images of my crew being torn apart invade my dreams. The next night I could hear them. And the third night, I heard the voice of the Darla leader whispering in my ear.

'Come to us.'

Everything I had fought against was now compelling me to take the ship back out there. I started suffering blackouts, and confusion. One minute I'd be prepping the ship to leave, the next I'd be standing over the unconscious body of one of my officers, having knocked him on his ass for trying to stop me. I heard the screams in my mind more and more frequently, and before I knew it, the Odyssey was three quarters of the way to the coordinates given to us by the Darla.

We reached the border of a large expanse of empty space, and aware of my actions, but unable to stop myself, I piloted the Odyssey over the line. All main power shut down instantly, like a cloud blocking out the sun. It was then that I realised I was not alone. I felt... a presence... a second consciousness trying to force its way into my mind... I...

I'm the last one left.

I managed to break out of whatever curse these things put me under, and steer the ship free under emergency power. The second I was out, main power came back, and I was able to set course away from that graveyard. I set course for an asteroid belt near Azanti Prime, and programmed the auto destruct to ignite if the ship failed to land there in the given time.

I will be teleporting to Azanti to attempt to live out my days there. But I can still hear them. I fear my days will be short lived. If anyone can see this recording... do not go looking for the Horizon.

Only blood lies before the Horizon.'

NINE

It had taken over an hour for the entire crew to come together on the bridge. After playing through Admiral Ransome's message twice more, Drusilla had reactivated the artificial gravity systems and managed to get a message out through the same console. Once assembled, she played the message once again for everyone else.

"Fuck."

The eloquent musings of Noah was the only word to be spoken for several minutes. As the screen went blank once again, Roman walked away and sat in the Captain's chair automatically, which garnered a few raised eyebrows from the others. He didn't notice though. In fact, he hadn't really taken much of Ransome's message that seriously. For him, he had reached his goal. He had the *Odyssey*. Mission accomplished.

"Sam, Noah, Dru, take your stations."

The looked at him slightly bewildered. Drusilla was first to speak to him, taking the First Officer's chair beside him.

"Roman, did you hear what he said? He buried this ship so nobody would find it. Do you really think we should stay here?"

Roman's face became steely and hardened, as he leaned in so his face was mere millimetres from hers. His eyes narrowed and he spoke harsh, and direct.

"I have spent most of my life hunting this ship down. And now it is mine. I don't give a shit if he buried it and I don't care about this... Horizon. All I care about is that we have the *Odyssey* now, and I'm not giving it up."

He then leaned backwards and repeated his command.

"Take... your... stations."

In that moment, Drusilla could easily have used her telepathic abilities to persuade Roman to order them to take a shuttlecraft instead, and leave the ship where it lay. But she knew she couldn't influence him forever, and once her presence was gone, he would simply be more motivated to return. She had wondered if this day would ever come, and had always feared it would mean the end of their close bond. Now the day was here. And Roman had changed. Another confirmation of that fact was what he said next, when she failed to move.

"I'm fairly confident I didn't make you a first officer, Dru. Get out of the chair."

In the background, Sam chose to look away and moved towards the helm, and Noah, after ordering the rest of the crew to report to the relevant decks, took his station at operations. Drusilla didn't break her gaze with Roman as she rose out of the XO chair and walked over to the tactical station next to communications. She turned away, feeling his cold eyes on her back, and inputted commands to combine tactical and communications into the one position. But her apprehension surrounding Ransome's message remained. There were still unanswered questions surrounding the bodies onboard, and what had happened to the Admiral after he left the ship. They did at least have a reason behind the continued power supply. Ironically, it was their chef who discovered it. Upon entering the galley which was situated near the main airlock, he found a regenerating power cell which had been wired into the conduits behind the kitchen, keeping all systems running. Who had done it, they could not say for certain, but it had kept the systems in pristine condition for the most part.

"Engines and star drive are online and seem to be in top condition."

"Let's run a couple diagnostics just to be safe, Noah. We've burned up one ship, I don't intend to lose this one to your incompetence."

Roman's words were cutting and sliced through Noah's nerves like a knife. He turned to face his Captain, but something had taken him over, like a shroud of darkness. He almost didn't recognise him, and decided now was not the time for an argument.

"Diagnostics confirm. Engines are fine... as I said," he spoke through gritted teeth.

Roman simply nodded.

"Sam, prepare to take us up and out. That is if you can handle something this big."

Drusilla was conflicted. She felt comforted that she was not the only one Roman was treating like shit, but she could not understand why. She tried to get a read from his mind, but it was almost like there were blockades in the way. He had somehow managed to slam steel shutters down all around his thoughts, and she simply couldn't penetrate them. But something was wrong with him, and she didn't like it. And clearly, neither did the usually obedient Samantha.

"What the fuck did you just say to me?" she yelled, spinning around in the chair.

"Watch your tongue, Samantha."

DAVID W. ADAMS

"Boss, you better be the one watching your tongue. Don't speak to me like something you just stepped in. I treat you with respect, and I expect the same back, or you can fly this bitch yourself. Clear?"

The bridge was silent, and Noah was open mouthed in shock. He decided he liked Sam even more than he already did, and made a note to ask her to the mess hall for coffee later. Roman, however, simply smiled.

"Perfectly clear, Samantha. You are relieved. Get off my bridge."

Noah's open mouth returned, and Sam spoke to protest, as did Drusilla, before Roman's booming voice cut them both off and echoed around the entire room.

"I SAID GET OFF MY BRIDGE!"

Sam shoved the chair aside, and stormed past Roman, fuming and consumed by anger and confusion. But Roman grabbed her wrist as she passed him, squeezing so tightly she thought the bones would break. He pulled her down towards him, and moved his mouth close to her ear.

"Next time I'll kill you."

Fear now rippled through Sam, something she had never experienced in Roman's company, and something she had never expected from him. He let go of her wrist which was already bruising, and stormed off the bridge, tears welling in her eyes.

"Noah, initiate take off procedures. Now."

Given the display of anger and violence they had just witnessed, nobody said anything else, and Noah simply nodded and moved over to the helm. Moments later, dust billowed around the *Odyssey* as she lifted from the floor of the asteroid, and the ship levelled out. The enormous window before them now became a viewscreen displaying vectors, and data down the sides and along the top. Roman watched, his eyes never breaking focus as they cleared the entrance of the rock, and entered open space.

"Course, Captain?" Noah asked reluctantly.

"Set course for the Saraswathi System. Maximum speed."

A look of confusion flashed over Noah's face, and behind them all, Drusilla matched it.

"I'm not familiar with that system, boss."

Roman nodded, and tapped in several commands to the panel on his chair. Noah's console then beeped at the receipt of coordinates transmitted to his station from Roman.

"Now you are."

The sarcasm cut the air just as everything else Roman had spoken since sitting in the Captain's chair, but Noah did as he was told and set course and speed. As the *Odyssey* star drive engaged, and the stars began to streak past, Drusilla tapped in the name of the Saraswathi System to the data banks. It took a moment for the information to come up. When it did, her eyes bulged. For someone who said they had no interest in locating the Horizon, Roman had plotted a course taking them right to it.

TEN

ALEXANDRIA DRAKE HAD SERVED ON SOME MIGHTY FINE vessels in her short but varied twenty-six years of life, but this one really did take the biscuit. She had never before seen a vessel of this age, let alone one in such incredible condition. Even by modern standards, the technology was high spec. Advancements had kind of slowed down the further the galaxy fell into emptiness. She was exploring every square inch of the main cargo bay when her maintenance colleague Dante Riverwood came through the bay doors. The expression on his face was not one of excitement and hope, and after a brief moment, Alexandria realised she was probably bordering on disrespectful behaviour.

"Hey Dante, any luck?"

Her colleague shook his head, and leaned against a large crate which according to the label, contained fresh fruit and vegetables. How fresh they would be after a hundred and fifty-odd years, remained to be seen.

"No doubt about it. We lost 'em."

The lost that Dante was referring to were their other colleagues in maintenance. When the engines had blown on the *Belle Vue* in mid-flight, inseparable working couple Daniel and Daniella Raymond had been inside one of the maintenance tunnels replacing deck plating. They'd been vapourised in the explosion. The third demise on the team had been that of veteran Crispin Tate. Crispin was the son of the captain of the *Northwestern* and one of the oldest surviving members of the second generation. When the call came in for the evacuation to the bridge, he simply hadn't been fast enough and although the crew assumed he'd been killed during a hull breach, in truth, his heart had given out just ten metres from the bridge doors as they closed.

"Sure gonna miss those guys," was all Alexandria could muster. She'd never been very good with sympathy, or any other emotions really. It had taken until the B*elle Vue* had crashed on Azanti Prime for her to start switching from an introvert to an extrovert. A process that was not yet complete. But Dante offered slight hope of new companionship.

"Yeah, well something is going on with Roman apparently. Just saw Sam charging down the corridor swearing and punching walls. Said he kicked her off the bridge. Given he seems to be in a mood, Matteo and Aliah decided to come down here. They're gonna switch to help us out."

Matteo Asher had been trained in weapons and tactical procedures. However, on the *Belle Vue*, he had served more time as an armoury officer, prepping and handing out the weapons rather than using them. With Drusilla taking the lead on away missions, and Sam dipping her finger into multiple pies of which tactical was becoming one, Matteo felt he was no longer wanted by Roman and the rest, but didn't manage to leave before things really kicked off.

Aliah Sunderland, on the other hand, relished in her supposed banishment from the bridge. She was originally the ship's main communications officer, before Drusilla came into Roman's life. She had harboured hopes that one day their Captain would fall in love with her and carry her off into a romantic nebula where they'd make babies among the stars. It soon became very apparent, however, that Drusilla, despite dating Hunter, had her sights firmly set on Roman Knight, and Aliah was transferred to engineering, specifically in charge of the communications array. Which never broke down. Not once. She was now delighted to join the maintenance team, and just moments later, joined Dante and Alexandria in the cargo bay.

"Hey guys! This ship is incredible! Did you see the simulation deck? The swimming pool? The officers quarters?"

Dante held up a hand to stop her there.

"Aliah, we just lost three people. Show a little respect."

Aliah's mood, however, failed to fade away. She simply nodded and began to take a look around, and after a few sneaky peeks into a couple of containers which housed basic nuts and bolts, she came across a capsule marked '*flight records*' and prised it open.

"Hey, what you got there?" asked Alexandria as she came practically skipping over. Dante followed slowly, much more acutely aware that they were meant to be checking for vital supplies and not snooping. If Roman was truly in a fowl mood, he would come down hard on them for this.

"Girls, leave it alone. That's not what we're here for."

"Oh come on Dante, live a little!"

Dante had lived a little. In fact, Dante Riverwood had lived a lot. Not counting scout ships he stole when he was a teenager, the *Odyssey* would be the twelfth vessel he had served on. A fair flight record considering he was only twenty-nine. He had not come into Roman's fold until two weeks before the crash, when he helped the captain escape from an ambush, and earned his respect. There wasn't much life left in the galaxy but what there was tended to surround trouble. And their captain always seemed to find it.

"Looks like minimised versions of the ship's flight plan, mission logs, encounters, star charts... it's like their whole journey is in this box."

Aliah handed a few data pads to both Alexandria and Dante, the latter placing them right back in the box they came from. He turned to leave.

"I'm gonna go find Matteo. He said he was checking with Alonso to see what supplies were already in the kitchen."

He left, without either of the women acknowledging him, as they were far to interested in how far the *Odyssey* had come and wanted all the details. Even in the twenty-fifth century, gossip still existed. But it was Alexandria who found the first pad mentioning the very thing Admiral Ransome had warned them about in his message.

"Hey Aliah, look at this."

The two of them sat shoulder to shoulder in front of the crate and scanned through a report they must have gathered from a member of the Darla on the initial journey.

'Mission log – date CLASSIFIED

Diplomatic encounter with a species known as the Darla, has proved to be rich in knowledge regarding the surrounding systems and the uncharted space ahead. However, the most peculiar piece of information provided, was rumours of a spacial phenomenon known as 'The Horizon.'

The Darla claim the Horizon, to be a point of energetic flux which ripples along the line of space time, allowing those who enter it to be transported back to a moment in their life when they were at their happiest.

The science officers have quickly dismissed the specific proposed nature of this phenomenon, but have not ruled out either the existence of the Horizon, or the potential space time link.'

The report was not signed, and the next three paragraphs were redacted and also marked classified, as was the report date.

"Why would they download the ship's logs into these pads and redact chunks of the information? If they wanted to get rid, why not just wipe the computer memory?"

Alexandria's question was a good one, but Aliah had no answer. She was already looking at three personal logs that mentioned the Horizon.

'Personal Log, Lieutenant Madeline Stockwell, date REDACTED.

Admiral Ransome doesn't understand. The Darla could be our guides to a new wave of exploration. We could not only explore space, but time as well. If we could only reach this Horizon, then surely the scientific ramifications would be incredible. Imagine going back in time before Earth was in conflict! We could stop the wars before they began!

It's a shame, he's too naïve and stubborn to see that.'

The next log was even more unforgiving.

'Personal Log, Ensign Carlito Santos, date REDACTED.

Ransome is a fucking moron.

The Darla can show us the way! There's no way he can tell me what to do. Barely keeps this shitshow running anyway. Always on the simulation deck enjoying holographic simulations of him returning to Earth some kind of hero!

I could go back. I could save her. If we took the ship to the Horizon, I could save my baby sister. She would be with me again.

I've heard others speaking the same way. If he's not careful, he's gonna have a mutiny on his hands.'

Aliah and Alexandria looked at each other, before turning

to the third log they had come across. The name on the top meant nothing to them, but the title did.

'*Personal Log, Commander Kelly Dresden, First Officer, date REDACTED.*

I tried.

I tried to warn Harry what would happen. But he let them on board anyway. The second I heard the Darla had telepathic abilities, I knew there would be trouble. But he didn't listen. And now three officers are dead.

I composed a message home for each of them, but we can't get the communications array back up and running. Ensign Santos thought it would be a way to convince the Admiral to head for this Horizon place. All it did was get him locked up in the brig.

And now the Darla are gone. Along with over a hundred crew members, and our escape pods. It's strange. When I'm asleep at night, I can hear their voices in my head. I didn't even known most of those who left, they were all of the lower decks, but I can hear each and every one of them in my mind.

I hear their screams.

Harry says he hears them too, but I've stopped listening to Harry. He's conflicted, affected by something else. One minute he's declaring we are heading away to a trade station, the next he's gonna blow up the ship, and then he's turning the ship back toward the Horizon. I don't know what the fuck he's doing.

I feel like I need to go there.

To the Horizon.

I can't explain it, but it's like the crew are calling me there. Like they need me, need help. And I keep thinking of my mother. Could I really go back and see her again? Could I stop her and Dad signing up for the Jupiter transports?

I need to know.

I need to get there.

I need to kill Harry Ransome.'

Aliah and Alexandria dropped the data pad at the same time, and it clattered to the floor.

"What the fuck."

Aliah's point was short and well made, eliciting a nod from Alexandria, who then responded.

"Do you think they killed him? I mean the dates have been redacted so we don't know if this was before or after he recorded that message on the bridge. Ransome said he's the last one, but what if he wasn't?"

Aliah was mulling her own thoughts though.

"I could see my Dad again."

Alexandria leaned forward to try and catch a glimpse of her colleague's face.

"Your dad?"

Aliah's voice changed, shifting down an octave or so, and Alexandria noticed a tear rolling down her cheek.

"I could see him again. We could be happy."

"Aliah, you're not making any sense. What are you talking about?"

Aliah now turned to face Alexandria with burning in her eyes and spoke through gritted teeth.

"Why won't he take us there? WHY?"

Alexandria started backing off. Aliah's eyes were now glazed over, and anger seeped from every pore as she advanced on Alexandria just as quickly as she was backing away, and continued her ravings.

"WE NEED TO GO TO THE HORIZON! WE NEED TO REACH THE HORIZON! I NEED TO SEE MY FATHER AGAIN!"

Alexandria, now full of fear, held her arms out and gestured for Aliah to calm down, and everything would be fine. As she did so, Aliah grabbed her wrist and with seemingly superhuman strength, jerked it all the way round in a three-hundred and sixty degree circle, snapping every bone within. Alexandria screamed with every fibre of her being, as Aliah did the same to the other wrist, and then continued to scream as her colleague scrambled across the floor towards the door.

"BRING THEM TO US! BRING THEM TO US NOW! WE ARE HUNGRY!"

The voice was now deep and harsh, the words with elongated 's' sounds, and the very decibels of the words vibrating the floor. Alexandria had misjudged her escape, and rather than finding herself near a door, her back slammed up against a maintenance conduit. A conduit she could not open with two broken wrists.

Tears streamed down her face, which was contorted in desperation and terror.

"Please! Please, no don't hurt me! Please!"

Aliah's face now leered at her, and crouched down.

"YOU WILL ALL DIE!"

With lightning movements, Aliah surged her hands forward, grabbing the top of Alexandria's head and her chin, before twisting sharply to the left and up. The snap of her neck reverberated through the metal walls behind her now lifeless body. Aliah turned away, seemingly in some kind of catatonic state, all evidence of the demonic presence within her now gone. Without knowledge, she slid several crates in front of Alexandria's dead body, blocking it from view, before walking towards the cargo bay doors.

When she got there, it was as if a light switch had been flicked. She blinked rapidly, confused at the tears on her cheeks, and wiped them away.

"Alex? Hey Alex, where are you?" she shouted aloud. "Hmm. Must have gone to find Matteo and Dante."

Aliah left the cargo bay, walking past a large floor to ceiling window as she did so. And as her reflection passed by, Darven's reflection looked back from the window, and smiled an evil grin.

ELEVEN

"Here, taste this."

Samantha cautiously looked at Alonso, but he gestured the spoon forward a second time, and she slid her mouth over the contents, and brought them into her mouth. The heat was instant, and her eyes started widening, her brow flushing red, and sweat beads began to trickle down in mere seconds. She spat the soup across the room spraying several surfaces, and lunged past Alonso to try and find some milk or ice cream to quell the fire now raging inside her mouth.

"Still too hot then?" he asked, removing the pot from the flames.

In between gulps of a chalky substance she had found in one of the cupboards, Samantha scolded him.

"What the fuck was in that Al? Damn near burned my face off!"

Alonso held up one hand in apology as he used the other to pour the soup into the disposal chute.

"In my defence, I have no idea what half these ingredients are. It looked like a sweet pepper. Just... purple."

Samantha had managed to calm her breathing down

enough to return her face to a normal colour, and she returned to her seat at the counter in the mess hall.

"Maybe don't feed this shit to the crew if you don't know what it is!"

Alonso smiled and leaned closer.

"Not thinking about what happened on the bridge now though, are you?"

That was a fair point. Samantha had stormed off the bridge in such a rage that she felt like ripping panels from the corridor walls, and hammering on the nearest training dummy she could find. When she realised she was almost to the mess hall, she ducked inside to find Alonso experimenting with the ingredients he had found. They had always gotten along well, and she felt that if she didn't share such a lot of similar interests with Noah, Alonso would be the ideal partner. He always listened and gave advice where needed. But something about this whole situation gave her the impression this was beyond even his sage wisdom.

"Something isn't right here, Al. Roman isn't himself. Hell even I don't feel like myself. I know he was out of line, the way he spoke to the crew, but I've never lost my shit like that with anyone, let alone the Captain. It was like something had a grip on my mind and then it was gone."

Alonso had kept himself isolate in the kitchen thus far, but had kept internal communications open so he was aware of the situation. He agreed it was damn peculiar. No scratch that. It was downright fucking weird. Firstly, the Captain was acting unusually in his behaviour. Then he claimed he had no intention of looking for this Horizon, only to set a course to the neighbouring system. But his real confusion came from his ingredients. Upon discovering the stash in the storage units within the kitchen, he found everything perfectly fresh or frozen, as if it had been picked the day before. It was true he had no idea what half of it was, but if this ship had truly sat here for over a century, how were these items so fresh, especially those that had not been in the freezers?

"I'm surprised Dru hasn't sensed something," he replied as he chopped what looked like a spring onion. "Her telepathic ways sure don't tell us a lot for someone who can read or influence moods and minds. Anyone would think she lied on her resume."

That made Sam laugh. It felt good. It was true that Drusila wasn't exactly forthcoming when it came to utilising her abilities, but Sam had seen them in action on multiple occasions. The effect was quite impressive. Wait... No that couldn't be it. She wouldn't do that, Samantha thought to herself. Would she?

Catching the puzzlement in her eyes, Alonso stopped chopping and tilted his head to the left.

"What is it?"

"It's just..."

"Go on."

"Do you think it could be Dru?"

Surprisingly, Alonso did not immediately dismiss the idea. In fact, he seemed like he might have already been thinking similar thoughts himself.

"Al?"

Alonso let out a sigh and placed both hands on the counter.

"You know about her and Roman?" he asked.

"They weren't exactly the best at covering it up," she replied sarcastically. "Fucking steam pouring out of the windows. Saw that shit all the way from the ship. Didn't help to see Dru's tits bounce past the window either."

The two shared a brief laugh at that. It was always those trying hardest to hide something that were the most obvious.

"Well ever since, they've been more fractious. I thought it might be because we finally found the legendary *Odyssey*. But she's done nothing to speak back to him, and he tore through you, her and Noah. I heard it on comms. And she didn't do shit. I just thought that was weird."

The more Samantha thought about it, the more she felt like there was a conspiracy of some sort building in her mind. The worrying thing was, there were factual examples to back up the theory. She exchanged looks with Alonso, who just shrugged his shoulders and then continued chopping.

"Al, do you really think-"

"*ATTENTION CREW OF THE USS ODYSSEY!*"

Roman's voice came booming through the intercom.

"*PREPARE TO ENTER CRYOGENIC STASIS. REPORT TO CRYO BAY 3. YOU HAVE TEN MINUTES TO DO SO.*"

Both Samantha and Alonso were confused. Cryo Bay? Was the Saraswathi System *that* far away? They didn't have time to think about it. Alonso switched off the power to the kitchen, and he and Sam made their way to the nearest lift shaft. As they descended to Deck 3, they said nothing, simply trying to figure out just what the hell was going on.

TWELVE

The bridge had its own cryo tubes built into the left hand side of the room, behind a series of emergency bulkheads. Roman had neither inspected them, or run a diagnostic to ensure they were still fully functional. There were, however, four of them. The bridge had been cleared except for Roman, Drusilla and Noah. Drusilla, however, remained at her post.

"I want you two in those pods in the next five minutes," Roman directed.

Noah turned around to protest, but when he saw the chiselled expression on Roman's face, unwavering, and resolute, he simply nodded once, and turned back towards his console. He was, however, going to run the highest possible diagnostic on those pods before he stepped anywhere near them. Drusilla, on the other hand, had not intention of getting inside. A point she finally decided to make clear to her Captain.

"What the hell are you doing?" she launched at Roman. "You say you're not hunting the Horizon, and then you set course for the star system next to its supposed coordinates.

You treat the crew like shit, you threw Sam off the bridge even though she's the best pilot in the galaxy, and you haven't left that fucking chair since you sat your ass in it!"

She took a series of deep breaths after that outburst, and Noah simply sat in his seat shocked at her outburst. Until that moment it had been quiet on the bridge, beside the usual beeping of instruments.

Roman's head turned slowly in her direction, and as his lips parted, Drusilla could see his teeth were clenched tightly. His muscles were bulging and his shoulders at maximum tension. Slowly, but purposefully, he rose from the chair and stepped down onto the deck.

"How DARE you!" he screamed, spittle flying everywhere. "You speak to your Captain like that? What gives you the GODDAMN RIGHT?"

Roman slowly began to advance on Drusilla, but she didn't move. Her plan was working.

"Maybe if you weren't such as asshole, we wouldn't have a problem!" she bellowed.

"Dru," began Noah.

"Shut the fuck up Noah!" she retorted.

Noah held both hands up and wheeled his chair slightly further away from the two of them. He had no intention of getting caught in any crossfire.

"Maybe we don't need some alien whore on this ship," Roman spat. "Besides, I've had you once, what's the point in doing it again?"

That one cut deep.

Drusilla's rage began to build inside her, but she quashed it back down, at least for the moment. She could not deviate from the mental minefield she was currently navigating through. She had felt something was not right with Roman ever since he sat in that chair. It had taken her a while, but she had detected a presence within him. A presence that *wasn't* him. And she almost had it.

"Or maybe," she retorted, "you've just gotten used to killing your crew at will. Nobody respects you anymore Roman. You're nothing but a waste of flesh and organs!"

Roman let out a fearsome roar, and swung his fist towards Drusilla's face. She ducked out of the way and Roman's fist collided with her control panel, sending glass and sparks everywhere. Drusilla ducked behind him, and leapt onto his back, placing the palms of her hands directly on each of his temples. She closed her eyes and began to focus hard. Roman began to thrash around, staggering from one section of the bridge to the next, slamming his back against a number of surfaces, impacting Drusilla's spine hard. She cried out in pain a number of times and on the fourth attempt actually felt something crack. She found what she was looking for.

In her mind, she saw a door. It wasn't shining or of the design of a ship's entrance way. It was old, battered and wooden. There were vines growing all around it, and in places, the green paint had flaked away, resting on the ground. The air around her was cold, and a gentle breeze tugged at her hair. She could feel her body taking a beating, but had to focus on this with everything she had. But she needn't have worried.

As Roman reached behind him, and grabbed hold of Drusilla's lower back, he gripped hard and attempted to pull her over the top of his head. There was a loud crack as an energy beam sliced through the air, and Roman staggered back into the wall, loosening his grip on Drusilla's spine. He shook his head trying to clear the disorientation. Another jolt hit him square in the shoulder, knocking him to the ground before a third strike hit him directly in the centre of the chest. Standing on the opposite side of the bridge next to an open panel marked 'weapons' stood Noah. He was in a stance of attack, and had fired the disruptor three times to take his Captain to the floor. And yet he still moved. As Roman's face contorted with anger, Noah calmly increased the power of the weapon to its maximum stun setting, aimed it at Roman's head and spoke softly.

"Sorry boss."

The weapon discharged as Roman lunged forward, but the impact of the blast sent him hurtling back through the air and into the same wall he had only just fallen against. Drusilla's body was slammed into that same wall, but Noah recognised what she was doing, and knew she would be fine. He holstered the weapon, and put out a ship wide announcement.

"All hands, belay the orders of the Captain regarding cryo-stasis. He has been relieved of command."

THIRTEEN

"How do you feel?"

The sweet and calming voice registered in Roman's ears, but his throat was so hoarse that he couldn't formulate a response. And his head was throbbing to the point of agony. Strangely, he felt like something was missing.

"I mean, personally, I think he looks like shit."

The unmistakeable voice of Noah dragged a wry smile on his Captain's lips.

"Maybe that's because my subordinate shot me four times with a disruptor pistol," Roman choked out as he opened his eyes.

The lights in the medical bay had thankfully been dimmed above his head, so they weren't too blinding as he sat up. He was surrounded by caring gazes and looks of concern. It was then that he noticed Drusilla lying on a medical bed opposite, eyes closed, and skin pale. Even her hair appeared to have lost its vibrancy.

"Dru!" Roman yelled, and launched himself off his bed towards her, his legs giving way momentarily beneath him as he grasped for the side of the bed. "What's wrong with her?" he cried.

Samantha moved to stand alongside him.

"She's in a telepathic coma of some sort. I haven't been able to break her out of it."

"A what? How is this possible, what can I do?"

Reluctantly, Samantha told him the truth.

"Roman, she's in this condition because of you."

His eyes were wild but no longer with anger. With fear. He searched his memory for what had happened but it was fragmented. He recalled himself shouting at Drusilla, but it had not been him. It was like he was locked behind a door of some kind, watching his mouth move and hearing the words, but unable to break free. He remembered every word he had said to her, and shame filled the voids where the fear had not reached. Then came the weapons fire and after that, nothing.

"Do we know what's going on with her at least? What is causing the coma? What was she doing to me before I went down?"

Roman's usually deep and gravelly voice was now croaking and breaking with emotion. Tears welled in his eyes and all of this only served to prove to the others in the room that the Captain they had witnessed since they entered the bridge had not been the real Roman. Samantha walked over to a screen which showed readouts of Drusilla's brain. She pointed at the patterns in turn.

"This is Dru's normal brain activity. It's basically the same as yours and mine. Slightly elevated when angry, more subdued when sleeping. There's no issue there. Underneath that, we have her telepathic brain waves. These operate at a much higher frequency than yours or mine. And they are very active. If these were normal human brain waves, I'd say she's having an argument, or a physical fight. They're spiking every few seconds, and I've had to give her a physical stimulant to stop her body from having reactionary spasms. But Roman, I'm not a physician. I know nothing more than that. I'm sorry."

Roman gazed down at Drusilla, and stroked the hair away from her face, cupping her chin in his enormous hand.

"I'm so sorry Dru," he said.

It was at this point that Noah joined them, and placed a reassuring hand on Roman's shoulder, which he grabbed affectionately.

"Roman, do you remember what you were asking us to do on the bridge?" asked Noah.

He thought for a few moments, and nodded.

"Cryo. I was telling everyone to get into cryo."

Noah nodded.

"Do you know why?" he asked.

"I... it wasn't me. It was like someone was controlling me. I was aware of the words, but not the comprehension behind them."

Noah sighed and nodded his head.

"Wait."

Roman's eyes sparkled briefly. He remembered something.

"What is it?" asked Noah.

Roman's face then contorted back to one of anger. Not at Noah, or Samantha or anyone else in his crew. But at the memory itself. He took a deep breath, and spat out only one word.

"Darla."

FOURTEEN

Non matter how much she tried, Drusilla couldn't move away from the door. She tried to take a step back, but ended up taking one forward. It was as if the door was magnetized and she was a piece of iron being slowly dragged towards it.

"Fuck it."

She stopped resisting and darted forwards, grabbing hold of the door handle, and turning it sharply to the left. The door flew open, and she felt surrounded by shadows and dark mist, swirling all around her. Long talons grazed her skin, slicing it where they touched, causing her to recoil in pain. But there were no discernible forms or creatures there. Then directly ahead of her, sat in the only piece of illumination, was a man. He was clearly not human, but resembled one, and was curled in a ball on what simulated a floor. The shadows and swirls moved above him, occasionally reaching out towards his body, leaving lashes behind.

Drusilla crouched down beside him, taking her out of the reach of most of the shadows, and saw she had at least ten lacerations on her arms and torso. And they were bleeding significantly.

"Hello?" she asked, as calmly as she could, wincing as she leaned forward to try and look at the man's face. "Can you hear me?"

The man's eyes shot open, and Drusilla staggered backwards a little, receiving another strike from above for her trouble. Blood now trickled down her face as she made her way back toward the man. She couldn't place what it was about him, but he seemed familiar to her.

"I... I can't stop them..."

The man's voice was quiet, muffled, and Drusilla barely heard him.

"Who? Who can't you stop?" she asked gently, placing a hand on his arm as she shook backwards and forwards on the ground.

"*Them.*"

He spoke the word with venom.

"Who is them? I want to help you but I need you to tell me who is doing this to you?"

"*I will show you.*"

The man darted forward, and gripped either side of Drusilla's head, and as he did so, a pain shot through her temple, immediately making her want to vomit. Images whirred past her eyes like a carousel of pictures and videos. So quickly she couldn't understand anything.

"Please... let go!" she cried out.

But the weakened man was putting all of his strength into his efforts, and one by one, the images and videos began to slow down and Drusilla started making sense of them. It went on for what seemed like an eternity, before the man let go, the images vanished, and the shadows began to descend towards the man's body. His breathing had quickened to the point of delirium, and as he watched the darkness come for him, he cried out once more.

"Stay away from the expanse!"

And with that, the doorway, the man, and the room all vanished, and Drusilla found herself sat bolt upright on a medical bed.

Samantha rushed over as the equipment started beeping. Drusilla noticed Roman was holding her hand, having fallen asleep beside her.

"Dru, Dru, I'm here," he said softly. "It's okay."

"No!" she exclaimed. "It's not okay! It's a trap!"

"What's a trap?" Samantha asked, slowly reaching for a sedative should it be needed.

"The Horizon! It's a feeding ground!"

Drusilla began stripping away the electrodes attached the her, and noticed the lacerations on her skin from her dream. They were *real*. Lifting up her shirt, she saw the gouge in her side, albeit now bandaged.

"They're waiting," she muttered. "Roman, we cannot go to the Saraswathi System. We have to turn back. NOW!"

Roman's eyes turned away from her, with him unable to meet her gaze. She noticed, and turned his head back toward her.

"What is it?"

Roman sighed before he responded.

"When whatever took over me... took over me, I locked everyone out of the controls. The flight path was sealed in and we couldn't break it open again. Noah tried, but he kept getting shot with electrical defences."

Roman nodded behind Drusilla, and as she turned, she saw Noah propped up on a second bed, with electrical burns running down one side of his face, one eye now milky white. He had taken a heavy assault.

"What are you saying?" she asked.

As if on cue, the intercom activated and the sound of Avery Smith's voice echoed around the room.

"Bridge to Captain?"

"Go ahead, Avery."

"We've just entered the Saraswathi System."

FIFTEEN

"Damn fucking cheek is what it is."

"Oh come on Lucille, you've been waiting for this chance for years. Now you got it."

"I am not a backup, Avery. I'm a first string player!"

The tension on the bridge had only gone one way, and that was up. With the 'first string' as Lucille had called them, otherwise indisposed, the engineering team had been drafted in to watch the bridge. Everyone except Carlos Rodriguez. He had been put in charge of the engines by Noah after he took his latest electrical charge to the face.

"Hey, Roman's got his reasons. Personally, I love flying this ship. It's so smooth and sleek."

Avery had always wanted to pilot one of these ships. He had dreamed of the day when the galaxy would restore itself and ships like these would be built once more. But of course, that day never came.

"You're not flying it though, are you Mr Smith?"

Lucille's reminder that the course was in fact locked in, took the shine off his moment. In truth, Avery Smith had been using the belief he was piloting the *Odyssey* to take his mind off the destination. He had heard the rumours going around the maintenance team about secret crew logs they had found, and mentions of the Horizon, and something referred to as the Expanse. But it was the disappearance of the people who had come this way previously that really shook his core.

Tatyana Martin, on the other hand, was an adrenaline junkie. She had suffered with a nerve condition which rendered her unable to fire weapons, and therefore unable to train for tactical missions, but anytime anyone needed an engineer in a dangerous place or on some perilous mission, and she was the first to volunteer.

"I bet there's nothing here but space whales and rocks," she said aloud from the communications station. "Don't you think if there was some magical place that could take you back in time, we'd have heard more about it?"

Samson London scooted out from under the console, having repaired as much of Roman's damage as possible.

"Space whales?" he asked with a raised eyebrow. "Where did that one come from?"

Tatyana jabbed his ribs with her foot.

"I'm just sayin' that if there really was something of value out here, it would have been plundered by now. The galaxy ain't exactly in pristine condition my friend."

Lucille scoffed at her colleagues.

"There isn't anything in pristine condition anymore. Sometimes I wonder if we're just existing rather than living at this point."

All three of the others turned and looked at her, each raising eyebrows in turn, before Tatyana broke the silence.

"That's deep. That's some deep ass shit right there. What you a psychologist now Luci?"

Tatyana's levity broke the tension, and giggles and laughter rang out around the bridge. Avery, being the team leader, decided to check in with the only member of the engineering section not present.

"Bridge to Carlos, how are things going down there?"

"Just peachy. A midsummer night's dream."

The sarcasm could not have been any sharper.

"Well we're still moving, so I'm assuming the engines haven't exploded this time?" Avery once again attempted levity, sensing tension in Carlos' voice.

"Obviously. All you gotta do is keep Noah away from them and they're sweet as a nut."

"Okay, well keep us advised of any changes my friend."

"Will do. Rodriguez out."

As the engineering stand-ins began to relax a little, Samson let out a grunt, and pushed himself fully out from the previously damaged console.

"Okay, that should do it. Viewscreen should be operational again."

Roman's enormous form slamming into the aforementioned panels had not only put the holographic overlay out of action, it had brought down an emergency blast shield, meaning the window was completely hidden.

"Okay, Tatyana, see what you can do."

Snapping her fingers, and cracking her knuckles, Tatyana made the dramatic motion of bringing her forefinger down over the panel, and tapping the one button required to activate the blast shield. With a minor groan, the door began to rise.

"Dramatic much?" Avery asked.

"Gotta have some fun," she retorted.

"We are not here to have fun," snapped Lucille.

A comeback was forming in Tatyana's mind, but she stopped, and the smiles dropped from all of their faces as the door lifted away into the roof of the bridge and they finally saw with their own eyes where they were.

The ship was completely enveloped by a golden cloud. The nebula shimmered in places, with mild lightning strikes in others, but the view was incredible.

"Wow."

Even Lucille was impressed with their new visage. It was achingly beautiful. They had seen their fair share of nebulas on missions, but being down in the engine room, they never usually got to see them first hand.

Samson, however, was not focussed on the nebula, but what was beyond it.

Nothing.

"Uh, guys?" he said rather hesitantly. "What's that?"

The others began to notice what he was referring to, and Avery squinted to try and get a better look at what lay beyond the nebula's outer rim.

"Luci? You enhance that for me?"

"I think so, hang on."

The image zoomed in dramatically, and the picture before them was now one of confusion. And fear. The edge of the golden nebula gave way to a small asteroid belt. Nothing like the size of the one where they found the *Odyssey*, but enough to require minor course corrections. But it was the vast emptiness that lay beyond the belt that had captured the team's attention. There were no stars, no planets, no rocks. Nothing. And certainly no space whales.

"Have you ever seen a void like that?" asked Samson.

"Only between your ears," replied Tatyana.

But despite the attempt at levity, even she had no commitment to the joke. Everyone's eyes were fixed on what was ahead of them. And that's when Carlos' frantic voice came over the comm system.

"Guys? We're speeding up! The engines are going to full impulse! I can't slow them down!"

It took the others a few seconds to realise Carlos was even speaking, but when they did, Avery frantically began trying to unlock the controls. On their present course, they'd impact the asteroids' smaller fragments. At a higher speed, it would cripple them. And right now, there were no visible corrections planned in the flight plan locked in by Roman. And no matter how hard he tried, Avery couldn't break the flight plan.

"Mother fucker."

SIXTEEN

"YOU NEED TO HEAR THIS!" DRUSILLA CRIED AS THEY ALL barrelled down the corridor towards the lift shaft.

"I understand that, but we need to get to the bridge first," Roman replied, now in his usual guise without influence, but slight notes of panic in his voice.

"You don't know what we're going into!"

Drusilla reached for Roman's shoulder, but missed and grabbed a handful of his long, dark hair instead, tugging him back to a dead stop. He spun around meeting her face to face.

"HEY!" he yelled. "I said, when we get to the bridge! No point in learning what you know if we're all dead before we hear it!"

A violent jolt sent them both careening into the wall, the sound of tearing metal audible in the distance. Roman steadied himself and stumbled over to a comms panel.

"What the fuck is going on up there?" he yelled.

But he got no response. He tried again. Still no response.

"Fuck this shit. We need to get up there, and fast."

They were almost there. So close. In fact Roman was just yards away from the entrance to the bridge. He could see the words written in white bold font, surrounded by a border of green paint.

BANG!

BOOM!

CRASH!

An impact of some sort struck the *Odyssey* with such force, the entire ship rolled, deafening sounds wormed around the entire ship. Panels blew out all along the walls, and both Roman and Drusilla were sent flying backwards the way they had come. As Roman peered through his swirling hair, he saw an enormous emergency bulkhead door slam down from the ceiling. He felt at least two ribs break in the impact of his body against the first bend in the corridor. As he slumped to the floor, he checked that Drusilla was alright. She had sustained a cut to the forehead but was otherwise mobile. Wincing as he stood up, he held his chest and slowly ambled his way forwards. The lights were now flickering intermittently, and smaller impacts rocked the ship, but nothing like the one that had struck just moments before.

In the emergency door was a window. Small, but enough to see the potential damage on the other side. It was this window that Roman was focused on. His gaze was locked. He could reach that door if he just kept his mind on that little window. Behind him, Drusilla noticed that the usual low thrum of the engines had ceased. Everything seemed much quieter than usual, and she could almost sense the pitch and roll of the ship, still moving forward, but also listing at the same time.

"Roman?" she called.

He swept a hand back signalling to hang on. He reached the door, and almost glued himself to it, such was the force of his intent to see to the other side. He clamped his eyes shut in disbelief at what he saw, throwing his head down resting his chin on his chest. He slowly moved his head back up to confirm his eyes were not playing tricks on him.

They weren't.

The doors to the room were hanging at either side, still attached but loosely. Almost as if clinging on to life. Jagged metal and conduits lined the entire recess all the way around the shape of the bridge. Sparks were flecking at random intervals, a small fire dying just to the left of the emergency door. Chunks of rock drifted by, as if they were balls on a snooker table and someone had struck them, scattering in all directions. It wasn't just that the room was empty.

The entire bridge, and everyone inside, was gone.

SEVENTEEN

THE SILENCE IN THE ENGINEERING ROOM WAS PALPABLE. In the event of the bridge being compromised, it was set up to function as a back-up command centre. But nobody had been speaking for almost an hour. The bridge was not only compromised, it had been destroyed. It was as if a great hand had swooped down and scooped if off the top of the ship.

"You know," Noah spoke, breaking the silence, "Tatyana asked me out once."

Drusilla, Samantha and Roman smiled and shared a couple of giggles.

"And how did that turn out for you?" asked Drusilla.

"She said I didn't have enough 'rizz' whatever that meant."

The levity was welcome and was the usual way this crew dealt with the death of colleagues. They knew they weren't out of danger, so they kept it light. Until it was time to go dark. And then they would go pitch black.

The brief respite and anecdotal relief ended when Matteo and Aliah entered the room with increasingly distressed faces. They had attempted to get scans of wherever the hell the were, and what lay ahead, but with main sensors taken out with the bridge, they were operating on slower secondary systems. And the news didn't make for pleasant reading.

"Okay, what do we have?" asked Roman.

Matteo took a deep breath and gave them all the ways they were fucked five ways from Sunday.

"Okay so the *Odyssey* has drifted into a small asteroid belt, and the flight plan that 'possessed Roman' plotted, didn't have any corrections for that."

A slight grimace from Roman, but he waved Matteo to continue.

"Anyway, sensors show we passed through a dense nebula on the edge of the system, which somehow managed to drain our shields in such a slow and meticulous way, that power levels didn't show a drain until it was too late. Then when the tiny chunks of asteroid hit, we were like a sitting duck. No shields, no way to alter course."

That explained the damage, but Aliah was ready with the pressing news of what was to come next.

"That, however, is the least of our problems. Directly ahead of us is an area of space that is referenced in the crew logs as 'The Expanse.'"

Drusilla's eyes widened and her head snapped up at the mention of that name. She had heard it in the warning message from Harry Ransome, and in her coma vision with the Darla male. She gestured emphatically for Aliah to continue, at which point she brought up a mobile holographic representation of where the ship now found itself, and began talking them through it.

"We are here, on the outermost point of the belt. The momentum of the engine burst was enough to keep us moving forward. However, we found... something else."

Noah screwed up his still scarred face in confusion.

"Something else?"

Aliah nodded.

"We've been able to send a small probe ahead of us by reconfiguring one of the torpedoes in the armoury. It found something."

She gestured her hand across the image and it brought up a vast array of purple, fuchsia and violet lights, all pulsing in a singular, almost straight line. At it's centre, burned a white hot filament. Everybody stared in awe at this incredible phenomenon, but nobody dared say its name.

"From what we can tell, it is a cluster of compressed spatial distortions, and the probe detected high levels of chronitons. Incredible high levels."

That got Noah's attention.

"Woah, woah, woah. Chronitons? Like time space distortion chronitons? Like... time travel?"

Both Matteo and Aliah nodded in unison.

"It's early to speculate, but it looks like there is some kind of flux going on at the centre of this string of energy. It keeps bouncing in and out of reality. Then it swallowed our probe."

"Swallowed?"

"Yeah. One minute it's sending confusing readings, and then as it began mapping out the size of the thing, it just went dead. No readings, and no further transmissions. Just gone."

That eerie silence crept back into the room as the information sank in. The Horizon was real. At least, according to their probe it was. The vibes shifted distinctly to the more positive, as if hope was somehow spreading through the ship, but Roman knew nothing was this easy. The hardships, losses, and battles he had gone through not only to simply survive, but to find this ship. Something like this was not about to be handed to them on a silver platter.

"What's the catch?"

Blunt, and to the point.

"The catch, is the Expanse," replied Matteo. "It's a 30 day crossing."

"30 DAYS!"

Samantha's first contribution to the discussion certainly brought everyone's attention to her outburst. Aliah continued.

"It's so vast in scale that going straight through the middle is actually the fastest way. In either direction port or starboard, it's eight weeks."

Drusilla offered the next question, even though she didn't believe the conviction behind her statement.

"Can't we turn back?"

Matteo had the answer to that. But it left Drusilla wishing she hadn't asked.

"We don't have the power or the shields to go back through the belt, and even if we did have the power, without shields, the effects of the nebula would weaken the structural integrity. Ship goes in, dust comes out."

A third bout of silence arrived, but Roman's mind was spinning. He still hadn't quite shaken off the effects of whatever had ensnared him earlier, and even though he was not in control of his actions, the guilt weighed heavily on his shoulders. His body had been used to send them on this course of destruction, and as a result, four more people were dead, and his ship, the vessel he had idolised as a child, was all but crippled. Despite his determination that everything would be better, his aura of death still surrounded him, drawn like a zipper across space. He finally turned to Drusilla, placed a delicate hand on her knee, and spoke softly.

"Dru, I think it's time we listened to what happened in that coma."

EIGHTEEN

"I thought that the Darla were all but gone?" asked Samantha, focussing on the mere existence of them than the harrowing details Drusilla had managed to piece together.

"So did I," she replied. "But this Darven was very much alive. Until whatever it was got a hold of him."

Roman was worried, more than he had ever been in his life, even growing up in a decaying galaxy with no real idea of his home world or where he belonged. But he wasn't worried about the warning of danger. He was worried about Drusilla. The story she told was of how a telepathic race had been coerced into using their abilities to control others. Drusilla, while still half human, held the same abilities. He wasn't particularly encouraged by the fact that Darven had been tasked with luring ships into the Expanse, either.

"Dru, I think we need to take some safeguards here. Whatever those things are that forced Darven to control me, could just as easily do the same to you."

Drusilla's initial response was one of immediate retort at the suggestion she couldn't take care of her own mind, but she quickly realised that Roman was trying to protect her. She nodded and thought back to some mental training she had undertaken in her youth.

"I can place mental doorways of a sort at various stages throughout my consciousness. If I should fall susceptible to attack, hopefully it will give me longer to fight back against whatever might be out there."

Roman was pleased with that, but had it been a realistic solution, he'd prefer her not to go through it at all. His further thoughts on the matter were interrupted however, by the sound of Alonso's voice coming over the intercom.

"Captain? Can you hear me?"

"Alonso? Is that you?" replied Roman.

"Yeah, sorry to bother you, but we got a situation down here in the cargo bay."

Roman looked at the others, who all shrugged. They had no idea either.

"What are you doing in the cargo bay?" Drusilla asked.

"I came to see if there were more food supplies. With the ship basically fucked, I wanna make sure we have enough rations."

Drusilla and Samantha nodded in agreement at the seemingly insignificant notion being incredibly valid.

"So what's the issue?" asked Noah.

The sound of a deep exhale came through the speakers.

"The issue is, behind my crate of sealed vegetables and pasta, there's a dead body."

Something akin to recognition flicked over Aliah's eyes, but dissipated quickly. Her mind had not been influenced long enough to leave a recognisable trace, and she had no idea of the evil she had earlier committed. Her reaction to the name, however, was genuine horror.

"It's Alexandria."

The sickeningly off centre angle of Alexandria's head caused Samantha to immediately run into the corner and vomit into an empty container. The skin around her neck was blue and purple as the bruising was developing. Her face was pale, and her eyes staring into the distance, a tear seemingly stuck on the edge of her left eye. But Roman was certain.

"A person did this," he snarled. "Somebody on this ship snapped her neck. I've seen this before. I've *done* this before. But I know I didn't do this. Which means somebody else did."

That put everyone else immediately on edge. How could they be certain that they hadn't been the one to do this? Darven could have inhabited any one of their minds briefly, forced them to kill Alexandria, and then released them. Ironically, it was Aliah who looked up at the ceiling, noticing the cameras, and made a suggestion.

"What about the internal security? Could we get hold of the footage?"

Matteo shook his head.

"The feeds only go to the bridge. It has the highest level of security, and the station was encrypted. There's no way to reroute the feed anywhere else."

Samantha scoffed.

"For such an advanced ship, the design of this thing was pretty stupid."

Roman immediately leapt to the *Odyssey's* defence.

"This ship was built over a hundred and fifty years ago. What would you expect? An old school security room with monitors everywhere and some dusty old fuck sat in a chair watching them all eating donuts?"

"Fair point. Sorry."

Roman nodded to accept her apology, and then turned back to Drusilla and Alonso.

"Please take care of her, and lay her in one of the crew quarters. Make sure it's hermetically sealed. Let her rest."

Waving his hand over Alexandria's eyes, he closed them gently, and allowed her body to be carried away. But his guard was now fully up. Any one of those he trusted could be a murderer, through no fault of their own.

"Hey," offered Noah. "If this Darven is dead, or gone, or whatever, that means we're good right? I mean there's no way any of us could get possessed now right?"

Roman thought about it, but his response wasn't exactly encouraging.

"How do we know Darven was the only one aboard?"

Back in the engine room, Noah and Carlos were now weighing up their best options. Roman wanted it in basic terms, so that's how they delivered it.

"We have two options, and to be honest, neither one of them is better than the other," Carlos muttered.

Roman sat up straight.

"Let's have it."

"Option One. We continue on our current momentum and see how far we get through this Expanse place. We have no idea how far we will get, but we will be able to conserve energy for later should it be needed."

Roman didn't like the sound of that, but despite Carlos warning him neither option was worse, the second one certainly sounded it.

"And Option Two. Direct ninety-percent of main power to an engine blast, fire us into the Expanse and travel further, faster. But then we'd be running dark on emergency back-ups for the rest of the trip. No lights, no lifts, no weapons, nothing."

Drusilla and Alonso came into the room just in time to hear the two options. Aliah had elected to go back to the cargo bay and inventory as many resources as she could that may be useful.

"So basically what you're saying, is either we hope for the best, keep the power on and see how far we get, by at which point we may have to blast the engines anyway, just with far less power. Or we blast the engines almost to max, and cut the power immediately, which leaves us confined to smaller areas of the ship and effectively a sitting duck?"

Carlos nodded at Drusilla's summary of the situations. Noah, however, was irked.

"What do you mean, basically. I got Carlos to say it basically."

Drusilla smiled, briefly at her friend, before turning to Roman.

"It's your call."

But Roman shook his head.

"No. I've got us into enough trouble as it is. This time, we all decide. Together. I won't be responsible for any more deaths."

He had never once been down to the maintenance hatches behind the engine room. Either on the *Odyssey* or the *Belle Vue* and yet Dante Riverwood knew exactly where he was going. As he climbed into the first hatch, he closed the door behind him, and his left hand gripped the disruptor tightly. His feet moved in rhythm to his heartbeat, his head fixed straight ahead, and his body rigid in it's stance. As he stepped over a large conduit running between walls, in the narrow space ahead, he saw a panel marked 'Life Support – Upper Decks.'

An almost demonic smile spread across Dante's face. He moved forward at the same pace until he was face to face with the panel. He reached forward with his right hand and ripped the panel from it's mounting, exposing a collection of wires and chips, which surrounded a central cylinder containing what looked like diesel fuel, but was in fact a purification fluid. This cylinder was responsible for making the air in the top half of the ship breathable. But it was no match for a direct hit from a disruptor on its highest setting.

Dante didn't even bother to step away. He lifted the weapon and placed the tip of it directly against the glass. The evil grin returned to his face, and somewhere behind those tortured eyes, the real Dante cowered in fear, crying out for help. But help would never come. As he felt his own hand press the fire button, he closed his eyes and thought of home.

NINETEEN

"REASSURING TO KNOW THAT EVEN ON LOW POWER THE goddamn sirens still work!"

Noah was running alongside Carlos, trying to keep his breath. The explosion had rocked the ship off course and caused it to deviate from a straight line. Their choices were now reduced to one option, but that would have to wait until later. With the fire suppression systems only working at sixty percent, they had to get those flames down as quickly as possible. In their current condition, they couldn't afford another hull breach. The extinguisher that Carlos was lugging behind him kept bouncing off his calf muscles and slowing him down.

"Come on Carlos, it's right up ahead!"

Carlos muttered something in Spanish under his breath towards Noah, but they both made it to the cargo bay door within seconds of each other.

"Hey, wasn't Aliah in here?" asked Carlos.

"Oh shit."

The manual release was fried, so Noah and Carlos had to force the door open by hand, and as the doors finally parted, they were almost hit by a dislodged roof beam coming down to strike the floor hard.

"ALIAH?" Noah shouted.

Carlos did the same, whilst putting out as many minor fires as he could find. The largest was on the far wall where there was an alternative entrance to the maintenance ducts. The door itself was blown clear, and the fire was emanating from the destroyed panel within. But it wasn't the panel that Carlos was transfixed by. Hanging limply from the fractured edges of the hatch were seared chunks of human flesh. As his eyes wandered around the horrific scene, he saw that there were what looked like cooked sausages fused to the floor panels, and around six feet from the fire itself, a dismembered and scorched human foot. But the foot wasn't male. It was *female*.

As Noah made his way over to his colleague, eyes wide, wanting to know why the hell there was still a fire burning, he saw everything. In various places spread out from the hatch in a six to ten foot arc were a series of body parts in various states of gore. Had it not been for the smell of continued barbequed flesh, the two men may have been trapped by the violent and hideous visage forever. Eventually, Noah grabbed the extinguisher and doused the flames. Without their presence, the horror was even worse than they had first realised.

Outside the hatch was the worst. Aliah's other foot rested on top of a container several feet away, and what looked to be her scalp was lying on the floor beside it, the hair still attached albeit deeply charred. Pools of liquid, previously red but now deep brown, surrounded the hatch doorway itself which now lay on its front, the blood cooked almost to solidification. Aliah had been standing on the other side of the wall, when the sabotage occurred. The blast had obliterated her.

Inside the hatch next to the former life support unit, were

a few more charred pieces of flesh, but an outline of a second person was burned into the next wall. The only evidence to that person's identity, lay fused to the ceiling above. It was the remnants of a breast pocket from a maintenance uniform. Even in it's burned and bloodied state, the name was clear.

Riverwood.

Under normal circumstances, accusations would be flying around at how one of their own could do such a thing. But not in this situation. Noah looked at Carlos. Carlos simply nodded. Leaving the horrific mess behind them, they briskly strolled through the cargo bay doors, and pulled them shut again. Given the time since the explosion, Noah figured they had only around a minute left. One minute to flee down four decks. Not possible. But it was their only choice. Pulling a mobile communicator from his pocket, Noah broke into a run, Carlos alongside.

"Roman! Can you hear me?"

A crackled response came through, but clear enough to make out.

"Go ahead Noah."

"We've got about forty-five seconds before the life support on the upper decks is gone. Get Alonso out of the galley!"

"Noah?"

"Yeah?"

"There's another one isn't there?"

Noah made it to an EV suit locker and prised it open.

"Yeah."

TWENTY

IT WAS SIMPLY NO GOOD. NO MATTER HOW HARD Drusilla tried, she could not get the terminal in the engine room to recall any data on the crew. She had been trying since they first boarded *Odyssey* and kept getting interrupted, and now they were about to go into emergency power and her chance would be gone. She rested her hands on her brow and closed her eyes.

"Who am I?" she asked herself out loud.

She paused for a moment, almost expecting an answer. But of course no answer came. She had no idea if her name was an indication of her lineage or simply given to her in tribute for some reason that she couldn't fathom. And now her only chance was about to vanish, amongst the uncertainty of survival through the Expanse. And what exactly lay on the other side, should they make it through?

Drusilla had given this a great deal of thought while the others were dealing with the sabotage. It was true that their modified probe had recovered data suggesting the Horizon did indeed exist, and that it had a large quantity of particles known to indicate a space time disturbance. But actual time travel? That seemed unlikely. And more so than that, how would such a phenomenon have the ability to target a moment in time related to an individual? There really was no way to know, but the thing she was certain of, was that one way or another, they had to reach it to find out. Only death lay behind them. The question they were now facing, was did death also lie before the Horizon?

She almost missed the transmission, Carlos' voice booming through the speaker beside her. She closed the information terminal down, and activated the comms.

"Go ahead Carlos."

"If we're going to do this, we need to do it now. If this thing decides to do any more sabotage, we won't have the required power to try it and we'll be stuck in the Expanse until we freeze to death."

"Or starve," she reminded him. Alonso had failed to discover usable resources in his trip to the cargo bay, and now it was in ruins, scattered with the semi-cooked remains of both Aliah Sunderland and Dante Riverwood.

"Yeah, thanks for the pep talk."

Roman, Noah, Samantha and Matteo came around the corner, and Matteo closed the doors behind them.

"Where's Alonso?" asked Drusilla.

"He insisted on going to the shuttle bay. Said he would use one of the shuttle cooking facilities if he had to. Didn't seem to care when I said all the shuttles had been totalled in the asteroid hits."

Noah's explanation made her feel uncomfortable. With everything going on, she had a high air of suspicion in her mind. Somewhere, there was another Darla onboard, but with no way of detecting them, they had no choice but to proceed.

"Okay, similar to Avanti Prime," Roman said before taking a brief pause as he remembered how disastrous that ended up being. "Fire the starboard thrusters and get us on a lateral path. Then cut the thrusters and fire the main engines. A burst of six seconds should do it. Let's not burn any more power than we need to."

Everybody tensed up. All five of them sat in a chosen seat, and gripped the arms of their chairs. Unlike the bridge, these all had seat belts. A welcome addition for Noah and Samantha, who had been flung from their stations on the bridge multiple times.

"Roman to Alonso. You good down there?"

"Yes Sir, got myself strapped into the *Rio Grande*. Nice place, one bed, one bath, half a kitchen. Vertically challenged, but not a bad little bedsit."

A comforting smile moved through the team, but dissipated just as quickly. The large monitor in the centre of the main engineering console had been repurposed as a viewscreen, and now each one of them stared at the darkness ahead. The absence of, well anything, was more chilling to them than what may potentially lurk within. Readings had come back multiple times of no visible lifesigns. But it was the 'visible' part that Roman was hanging on to. Just because they can't see them, doesn't mean they aren't there. But regardless, this was it.

"On my mark."

Drusilla hugged her body against her chair even tighter, and both Samantha and Noah double checked their seatbelts.

"Ready, boss."

Samantha had inputted the flight plan, and locked it in. The helm had been set to automatically correct any deviations caused by an outside force. This would of course send them crashing into anything in their way if they tried to avoid it, but given the peril they were already facing, the crew determined it was a worthy small risk.

DAVID W. ADAMS

"Fire the starboard thrusters."

"Starboard thrusters engaged."

Three seconds ticked by very slowly.

"The *Odyssey* is now in position boss."

"Cut the thrusters, and stabilise with the port set."

"Minimal fire from port thrusters, we are now lined up with the centre of the Horizon at the other end."

"Well, this is it people. Any last words?" Roman asked.

Noah swivelled round.

"Nobody is allowed to die before me. Otherwise I get terribly lonely."

Roman admired his friend's humour in the moment, but Noah was not alone.

"If we survive this, and you throw me off the bridge again boss? Imma beat your ass."

Samantha even made the usually stern Matteo laugh with that one. He himself offered no words of wisdom. Drusilla took the tone down to a more serious level and gave a sombre address.

"I know we've lost a lot. And we might not make it through this in one piece. But I just want to say to you all... thank you. For taking me in, and making me feel less of a freak and an outcast. I love you all deeply."

Of all the people in the room, it was again Matteo who broke his usual approach, and Samantha caught him wiping away a tear as she did so herself. Roman was last. He thought about what he should say. How he should thank them all for sticking by him. How they had saved him from incredibly dark places on many occasions. How he loved Drusilla deeply. And how he hoped he would see them all on the other side. But he didn't. Instead he said just two words.

"Hit it."

TWENTY-ONE

It was a very different sensation this time around when compared to the manoeuvre at Azanti Prime. The force from the far more powerful engine of the *Odyssey* felt like it had launched them through an entire galaxy in moments. The forces on their bodies was to such an extent that each one of them had passed out from the exertion. After a burst of six seconds at full speed, the engines had disengaged and powered down, all non-vital areas had been sealed and deprived of breathable air, and all of the main lights began to switch off.

CLUNK. CLUNK. CLUNK.

One by one, each corridor throughout the ship went dark.

CLUNK. CLUNK. CLUNK.

A few moments later, the emergency reserve power kicked in, and every corridor still open to the crew began to glow and pulse a harsh red. It was an appropriate colour for the level of danger they now found themselves in. The engineering room was bathed in a white glow, a conscious choice from the shipyard team during construction. They felt if there was an emergency, white light would be much more suited to repair work than dark red. When the decision had been made all those years ago, it was commented on why exactly that couldn't go for the rest of the ship. Evidently they were overruled saying red gave the impression of danger and reinforced the severity of the situation.

Nevertheless, Roman was very glad they won out in at least this one room as he began to stir. Every part of his body ached as if he'd been in a twelve round fight with a prized boxer, but the pain extended to his extremities as well. He slowly opened his eyes and got his bearings. Nobody else had yet regained consciousness, but on brief inspection, they all appeared to be uninjured. He moved to activate internal comms to check on Alonso, before realising they too were now offline. He would just have to take care of himself for now.

Cautiously moving over to the panel displaying the makeshift viewscreen, Roman saw nothing. He checked to make sure the display was in fact still operational. The machines were not at fault. There was simply nothing to see. Incredibly unsettling for someone who had lived among the stars his entire life. He found himself staring into the monitor, his eyes mere inches from the screen.

There. What was that?

Roman thought he had seen some sort of displacement. The darkness appeared to have shifted just for a moment. The kind of shift a cloaked object would make as it moved away. The thought made his blood run cold. But after several more minutes of staring, he saw no evidence to suggest there was anything but a void.

"What are you looking for?"

The voice immediately behind him, and the hand on his shoulder made Roman scream out loud and jump to the side, where he bumped into Noah who made a disgruntled sound to express his displeasure.

"Jesus, Dru. You trying to make me shit myself?"

Drusilla found it hard to keep a straight face. It had not been a common occurrence to catch their captain unawares, and should they survive this trip, she intended to never let him live it down.

"How are we looking?" she asked.

"See for yourself," was Roman's reply, pointing at the empty screen.

Drusilla stared into the same screen for a few moments, as equally bewildered as the Roman, before turning away and joining the others who were now fully conscious.

"So, exactly how long are we stuck like this?" Samantha asked, still hoping the initial time frame was on the pessimistic side.

"You know how long, Sam. Thirty days and a few hours."

Roman cut through the hope with a very sharp knife, and Samantha slumped back into her chair.

"So what do we do for the next month? Besides keeping an eye on the flight path, there is literally no maintenance to do, no computers to read or watch TV on. And most of the ship is locked down."

Roman hadn't really put much thought into what they would do, only the requirements to initiate the plan. What he wanted to say was that they would likely spend most of the trip hunting or falling victim to the remaining Darla. They may already be in the Expanse, but chances are, this mysterious passenger would not want them to leave. But, as usual, he spoke words different to those he felt.

"Well, first port of call should be to check on the others. Matteo and Noah, head down to the engine bay and make sure Carlos is okay. Me and Sam will go check on Alonso and see if he prefers the real estate up here. Dru, keep an eye on the flight path."

Each of them nodded in turn and tried their hands at the manual releases on the doors for the first time. It was not light work, and both teams had at least six of these doors between them and their objectives. Still, at least it would save them going to the ship's gymnasium in the dark.

As they closed the doors behind them, Drusilla pondered a great many things. Would she ever find out who her parents were? Would they be able to stop the ship once they reached the Horizon. *If* they reached the Horizon.

And of course, the number one question on her mind.

How long before the crew found out that she was the one who killed Dante and Aliah?

TWENTY-TWO

WAKING UP IN THE DARK WHEN YOU HAD GONE TO SLEEP under the glare of overhead lights was certainly unsettling. Even the blinking warning on the controls of the shuttlecraft weren't enough to assuage Alonso's fear of the dark. Particularly as the shuttle was upside down. As he struggled not to lose the small lunch he had eaten earlier in the day, he fought against the restraint of his seat belt, trying to tear through the material where it had frayed slightly. Alonso had not escaped the engine burst effects whilst residing inside the *Rio Grande*. The craft had already been at an askew angle when he had boarded the ship, but as the forces of the sudden burst took hold, and the ship slid to a complete one-eighty, random items from the overhead compartments had rained down upon him, and his face looked like it had been beaten with a sledgehammer.

His left eye was almost completely swollen shut, and he had a large gash in his right eyebrow, with only his reverse posture preventing the blood from dripping into his eye. His lip was also split in two places, and he could taste copper in his mouth. He couldn't be sure, but he felt as though his nose was broken, and there was a distinct pain in his collarbone. Fractured, most likely, was his initial thought.

"Goddamn fucking seatbelts!" he roared, getting more and more frustrated, the more energy that was expended.

Alonso managed to reach into the pocket of his chef's coat, which was now far from white, and splattered with his own blood. He could feel the flat plastic edge of his tomato knife, and just got enough of a grip on it, to free the blade. He wasn't sure what good it would do. It was completely flat, with a small area of serration running from the mid-way point to the tip, which then curved round into a blunt surface. While the small serrated area was razor sharp, it didn't lend itself to prying things open. But it was all he had, and so with careful motion, he slid the rounded tip of the knife into the clasp holding the belt in place, and started to jimmy it left and right. It felt as though he was getting somewhere, and so he increased the pressure on the knife. But the blade was incredibly thin, and after one push too far, the blade snapped in half, the remaining serration slicing through Alonso's thumb, before continuing it's trajectory through the nylon-like material in the seatbelt. As he screamed in the pain from the cut, Alonso was freed from the belt, albeit not in the way he had intended, and he slammed into the roof, hard, before somersaulting down the slight incline, coming into contact with the rear door.

"Mother fucker!" he screamed, as his body screamed in pain.

He looked back up at the shard of blade still stuck in the seat belt clip, which was now dangling haphazardly from the seat, and the other piece on the roof, which was now of course the floor.

"Cheap goddamn alien steel! That's the last time I buy an Earth replica!"

The rear of the shuttle was much darker, with no warning lights providing any kind of illumination. But Alonso's reason for being in the shuttle instead of the bridge in the first place, had nothing to do with suspected safety, potential supplies, or even a botched escape attempt should he suddenly need another way out of the ship. From his other pocket, he removed a small electrical tool akin to an old fashioned screwdriver. On the handle end, was a button. With one click, Alonso depressed the button, and the end of the tool burst into life, illuminating a five metre radius. The light itself was completely circular, shining light in a three-hundred-sixty degree arc. As Alonso scrambled across to a large panel marked 'EV Suits,' he extended the tip of the tool beyond the mount of the light, and inserted it into a hole in the top corner of the panel. A few turns later, and a screw fell to the floor and rolled away. He repeated the step three more times, wincing as he put pressure on both his sliced thumb and his collarbone.

Once all the screws were out of place, he pulled the panel free, and placed it carefully against the rear hatch, shining the light inside the now open hatch. A look of relief spread across his face as he saw his contraband had not been discovered. Reaching forward, Alonso pulled out seven bags of white powder, each containing approximately one kilogram in weight. He began to smile, as he pulled one of the bags free.

"Thank fuck for that."

Checking over each of the bags in turn, making sure they had no splits or tears, he placed them back into the compartment, and relaxed against the rear door. He had taken a huge risk searching through the containers in the private crew quarters, but as soon as he found those drugs in one of the security officers' lockers, he had felt the payoff was worth it. Alonso was a reformed criminal, but for the right money, he was willing to dabble. In a dwindling galaxy of life and resources, there were plenty of people who wanted to take away the pain, but weren't willing to take their own life, and Alonso was willing to take their money and render his assistance. When he realised the level of this mission, however, he decided to smuggle it in an empty food container to the shuttle bay, and chose the shuttle that had the least damage, but the most impression of being difficult to return to its upright position. The EV suit had been moved to one of the containers which had ironically smashed him in the face. Now though, he knew he had to return the narcotics to their hiding place.

"Now where the fuck did those screws go?"

Shining his torch around the floor, he found three of them lodged not far from his feet in the groove between the door and the floor. But the fourth one was nowhere to be seen. He screwed the three in place, having replaced the panel, and began searching for the final screw. He knew if they got out of this, and the last screw was missing, it would arouse suspicion. The screws had a grey cover attached which hid their presence once in place. One missing would draw the eye.

Alonso dropped to his hands and knees, and moved methodically along the roof/floor with his light. Suddenly, there was a thud from the other side of the door. Alonso's eyes flew up, and he shone the torch at the door. He took a breath, and listened. Nothing. He returned to his search when another thud, this time louder, vibrated the shuttle. Again, Alonso stopped and looked at the door.

"Roman?" he asked into the darkness. "Noah? Sam? That you?"

Silence. His own blood was thundering in his ears, and the quiet was consumed by the sound of his own heartbeat. Sweat began to bead on his brow. Alonso was not a stupid man. He knew the second thump had been closer than the second. So he waited.

THUMP!

And then he started to count.

"One... two... three... four..."

THUMP!

Four seconds between thumps, and each time they seemed to get significantly closer. Alonso then heard a scratching noise, like nails on a chalkboard, and his hands flew to his ears. As he did so, he dropped the torch, which rolled away from him, and as his eyes began to focus on it, it fell through a gap between the door and the roof/floor that he had not noticed was there before. The top of the door was *pulled back*. Only slightly, but enough to see the light on the multi-tool sat on the shuttle bay floor around ten feet away where it had rolled and come to rest. He gently nudged the gap with his foot, and found it opened wider. He couldn't tell if it was the scratching that had opened the door, or the impact of the fall the ship had taken, but one of the tritanium hinges had sheared off. At a push, Alonso could sneak through, retrieve his multi-tool, and secure the drugs before the others came looking for him. He knew it was a huge risk, as established, he was not a stupid man. But he was greedy. The money from those drugs would get him his own ship, and he would be able to make a real living instead of working for meagre compensation cooking meals for the higher ups.

The fifth thump sounded further away, which ordinarily would arouse more suspicion. But Alonso was creating a calculated plan to secure his investment, and saw it as a blessing. Slowly but surely, he squeezed himself through the gap in the door, and lowered himself down the side of the small craft. But the drop was too steep. He was clinging on to the lowest part of the vessel, and was still dangling at least twelve feet in the air. There was nothing for it. As Alonso let go and fell towards the ground, movement caught his eye somewhere above him, and momentarily took his attention. That split second was all it took. Paying no mind to his targeted landing, or controlling that landing, he hit the floor before he knew it, and the snap as his ankle bent inwards, echoed around the shuttle bay, followed immediately thereafter by his blood curdling scream.

Alonso rolled onto his back, trying to keep his leg off the floor, but the weight of his now virtually severed foot pulled on the breakage, and the blind pain almost caused him to pass out. In the small glint of light reaching him from the tool, which was still metres away, he saw a bone protruding through the skin, and blood beginning to pool around him. His head swooned and his mind felt as if it was floating. All the while, he was sat in complete darkness, the only light on his multi-tool.

THUMP!

Alonso swallowed his cries of pain as he was snapped back to attention. He clenched his jaw trying to suppress the pain stabbing throughout his body, his head pounding with both agony and fear. Sweat trickled down his face and into his lower back. His eyes scanned the darkness, but any view of potential shadows was blinded by the incessant light from his multi-tool.

THUMP!

Whatever it was, was considerably closer. Alonso felt eyes all over him. Watching. And then something else. His breathing was the only sound he could hear, and it was getting harder to listen past it. Against his body's better judgement, he held his breath for a moment. But he still heard breathing somewhere behind him. Harsh, rattling, almost animalistic breaths snarled somewhere in the blackness. Alonso shifted his weight to the other side of his body as carefully as he could, in order to turn around. Three-quarters of the way round, he closed his eyes tightly, took the deepest breath yet, and span to face whatever it was sharply, jolting his ankle in the process. There was nothing there. The breathing was gone. No noises, no breaths, no nothing.

Don't make a noise, he kept telling himself. Stay quiet. Slow your breathing. But his body betrayed him. Involuntarily, he shouted into the empty nothingness before him.

"WHERE ARE YOU!"

Alonso then couldn't stop himself from dragging his way forward towards the multi-tool, each movement agonising, leaving a bloody trail, and the sound of the bare bone scraping against the cold steel of the floor sending a shiver throughout his body. He touched the edge of the tool with his fingertips, almost collapsing with the effort he had expended to get there. The light moved in its arc as he did so. But one triumphant push later, he gripped the tool in his hands. An urge tore through him to release a victorious cry.

"FUCK YEAH!" he roared.

He thrust the tool upright into the air in achievement, but a second cry of joy never came. The light briefly flashed across what looked like jagged and yellowed teeth, the and was reflected, shining in drool. In return, it luminated the fountain of blood now pouring from Alonso's mouth and down his now crimson stained chef coat. His body convulsed violently, as he forced his eyes to look down and witness the long, black, razor tipped tail now protruding from his abdomen. The impact had been so swift and powerful, that Alonso hadn't even realised he was now several feet off the ground. The floor of the shuttle bay was now glistening with Alonso's blood, and with an equally swift movement, the tail receded from his body. His blood and organs cascaded to the floor in a sickening torrent of viscera, followed moments after by his body, which crunched loudly on impact as the rest of his bones gave way. As the final throws of death seized his body, Alonso remained alive just long enough to see a pair of glowing red slits in the darkness, and an open, needle lined mouth coming towards him.

TWENTY-THREE

Being in such close proximity to the engines normally, would have them covering their ears and trying not to look at the lights, but the engine bay in its current condition, was not overwhelming. It was creepy. Matteo had never seen an idle engine in all the years he had spent onboard ships and freighters. This had partially stemmed from the fact that the engine bay was incredibly claustrophobic. Unlike the spacious engine room or main engineering as it was often referred to, the engine bay was a long and narrow passageway, with a catwalk either side of the engine core itself. The ceiling was low, and the floor was a metal grate suspended over a vast drop into the fuel reserve tank. For safety reasons, the engine bay was usually sealed, but it was the only place to initiate such an overload of energy, and so Carlos had needed to be present at the time of the burst. The danger was not insurmountable. There had been risk of internal fracturing, and Carlos being fried by the resulting explosion. However, given their survival, albeit whilst unconscious, Matteo mused that Carlos must have remained in one piece. It did not occur to Matteo to look behind him as he made his way along the port side of the catwalk. If he had utilised this small action, he would have noticed that Samantha was no longer behind him. Navigating the corridors in a blackout was no small feat, and their unfamiliarity with the ship's internal layout was also hindering their progress. Somewhere along the way, Matteo turned left and Samantha had turned right. Only Matteo had managed to locate the entrance door to the engine bay.

"Carlos!" he called down the tunnel. "Carlos?"

His words echoed momentarily, before they dissipated. Neither call of the engineer's name garnered any kind of response. Instinctively, Matteo reached into his pocket and pulled out one of the mobile communicators. Of course they ran from internal power and were not functioning.

"Worth a try," Matteo muttered to himself. "Hey Carlos? Where you at man?"

As Matteo crossed the half way point of the catwalk, he noticed just ahead of him, noticeable in the dim glowing red light of the emergency fixtures, one of the grates missing in the flooring. Expecting the worst, Matteo drew his disruptor from his waist, and held it tightly, keeping it pointed down in case his reflexes got the better of him. A faint jingling sound was coming from ahead of him, seemingly around the place the gap was situated. It was a sound of metal on metal, and followed no distinctive pattern, simply randomly chinking against the deck plate.

It was not until Matteo reached the hole in the flooring that he saw what was making the sound. Dangling from the edge of the neighbouring grate was a metal hook, which in turn was attached to a long nylon strap. And at the end of that strap, was Carlos.

"Holy shit! Hang on Carlos!"

The strap in question was that of Carlos' engineering bag,

which had now wrapped around his throat and was slowly choking him to death. In truth he was fortunate not to have snapped his neck when the deck plate fell, but lifting him up would be no mean feat.

Carlos' face was turning purple, visible even in the scarlet light from above, and pulling on the strap to lift him up would surely finish his breathing for good. Matteo therefore devised a clever solution. He reached behind him, and ripped a cover off a section of the main engine. Being offline, they provided him with a safe source of potential salvation. Tearing with both hands, he ripped a bundle of optic cabling from within, and wrapped one end around each of his wrists, and dangled the lengths of cable down into the hole.

"Carlos, grab hold and I'll pull you up! Hurry!"

With dwindling oxygen, Carlos barely managed to grab hold of one of the cables, but it would suffice. Matteo pulled with everything he had, steadying his feet against the hand rail of the catwalk to ensure he didn't follow the same fate. The cable strained against the weight, but inch by inch, Carlos began ascending upwards, and the tension on his neck began to ease. When he was within six feet of Matteo, Carlos managed to garner enough strength to grab the second cable, making the job infinitely easier on his colleague. That was until he was hit in the face with a sticky, jelly-like substance landing right between his eyes.

"What the fuck?" he managed in low raspy breaths that Matteo couldn't hear.

He shook his head from side to side to try and shake the goo from his face. And when he looked back up, his face contorted with terror. In the pulse of the emergency lights, Carlos saw, directly above Matteo, perched on top of the engine itself, was a hunched figure of some kind. He began gesturing wildly towards Matteo, who was almost in reach, but his words would not come as his throat burned from the strap of his bag, and Matteo took his flailing limbs as a sign he was in trouble, simply trying to pull faster. However, when the lights next pulsed, the figure was gone. Carlos began to suspect he was imagining things from the lack of oxygen, but continued to look around in every direction. One minute, he felt eyes to his left, then to his right, and bizarrely, even beneath him, as if someone was looking up waiting for him to fall.

Finally, after what seemed like an eternity, Matteo's hands clasped around those of Carlos, and the engineer was hauled back up to safety. Both men collapsed against the side of the engine dragging in as much breath as their lungs would hold. Carlos used his hand to wipe across his forehead, and began to examine the sticky substance between his fingertips. If he didn't know better, he would have assumed it was drool, such was the viscosity of the liquid. Matteo, having finally caught his breath, noticed this, and leaned closer.

"What the hell is that?" he asked.

The movement was so quick that the whooshing sound didn't materialise until after the impact, confusing Matteo completely. With his own face mere inches away, Matteo watched as four paper thin lines began to appear horizontally along Carlos' face. Four seconds later, the top of Carlos' head began to slide towards him. That was followed by the second, then the third. As the bottom half of Carlos' jaw slid away from the rest of his body and slopped onto the grate beside Matteo like raw meat on a slab, Matteo screamed with everything he had.

Scrambling backwards, Matteo's right hand slipped into the hole he had just pulled Carlos up through, and he was able to catch himself. His disruptor plummeted downwards, however, but he did not hear it land in the empty fuel tank.

What he heard pierced his very soul. An incredibly high pitched roar echoed up the chamber, and as he squinted, he could see red slits in the darkness below. Two. No, six. Then he noticed at least a dozen more. No, not slits. They were *eyes*. Dozens of red eyes all staring back at him, and their shriek was like that of a banshee, only a hundred times louder. Had his hands not been firmly gripped to the railings beside him, Matteo would have covered his ear drums.

Another whooshing sound beside him and he looked just in time to see two sets of four talons tear into Carlos' shoulders, the razor sharp tips digging through his skin as if it was merely paper. The pressure applied was enough to spray Matteo's face with the still warm blood of his dead friend. Pressed up against the roof of the catwalk, Matteo could make out two more of those red eyes looking down at him, and in one swift motion, the rest of Carlos' mangled body was dragged away into the darkness in the time it took Matteo to blink. A breeze rushed past him, and given the low ceilings of this place, he knew it was inches rather than feet away. He wasn't about to die here. He scrambled to his feet, leapt over the missing grate, garnering more tortured screams from below and sprinted as fast as his legs could carry him to the opposite end of the catwalk to which he had entered.

He reached the opposite exit door, but behind him, he could see red glows bounding toward him. He punched in the code, but two of his fingers mashed the keypad and an error beep screamed in his face. The deck plates were now shuddering with every thunderous step these creatures took. A second wrong code entry. Closer and closer they were to slicing their way through their second body in as many minutes. The third attempt failed too, Matteo simply too traumatised by his experiences to input the correct code. This was it. He was out of time. He turned to face the creatures, and waited with his eyes closed. The thumping of their approach got louder, the vibrations more intense.

"May God have mercy on my soul."

A tail lashed out ahead of the first creature, but alongside Matteo, the control panel beeped an affirmative noise, flashed green, and the door slid open. Samantha grabbed hold of Matteo's remaining hand and yanked him through the doorway, typing the code in once again in lightning speed, slamming the door shut.

She closed her eyes expecting the creatures to smash into the door. But the impact never came. All was once again silent. She turned her attention to Matteo who was now lying on the floor, blood pouring from his severed left hand, his breathing quickening with each passing second.

"Ah shit, hang on Matteo!"

Samantha's voice was distant, and growing ever more so, as Matteo's eyelids became heavy. As he lost consciousness, his mind replayed the images of Carlos' head being sliced up like a Sunday roast, and the evil, demonic grin of the creature standing behind him as it liked the sprayed blood from its lips with its tongue.

TWENTY-FOUR

3 DAYS. IT HAD BEEN 3 DAYS SINCE ANYONE LAST DARED venture out beyond the engine room. Drusilla had kept the door sealed whilst alone, and had only opened it upon hearing the distressed voices of first Samantha and Matteo on the other side, and then Roman and Noah's voices after their discovery of whatever was left of Alonso in the shuttle bay. Matteo had spent almost thirty-six hours drifting in and out of sleep, his arm now wrapped in blood soaked bandages, Samantha's belt still fixed tightly around it. She was still having moments where his screams as Drusilla cauterised the wound with a medical tray she had heated with her disruptor, reverberated through her mind. The only part worse had been the brief but nauseating scent of cooked flesh as the treatment had been applied.

They had determined between them, that whatever had boarded the ship had done so whilst the engine ports had been open. That was the only way they could get onboard without detection, even with emergency power on minimum. After the engines burned out, there was a thirty second period where the vents moved from a wide open position to closed.

Samantha had also speculated, after a coherent hour or so with Matteo, that this was why there were seemingly dozens of them in the catwalk.

With the upper decks out of bounds after the sabotage of the life support system, the cargo bay potentially home to more of the creatures, and enough food and medical supplies in engineering to sustain them for over a week, the decision was made to lock everything down.

"Can we tell how far we've travelled yet?"

Roman's usually gravel-tinged voice came out weak and horse. The man was breaking. Every time he swore nobody else would die, they inevitably lost someone else. He had tried his best to bear the brunt of this without showing any form of weakness to the crew, but he was failing. He knew Drusilla could read his mind should she choose, but he was grateful that she seemed as pre-occupied as he was.

"Four days travel, give or take an hour. So at this point, we're just short of a sixth of our way through the Expanse."

Collective sighs filled the room at Drusilla's reply. Not even a third of the way across and they had lost two people, and had effectively a third man down. Matteo was in no shape to do anything more than lie there. And right now, Roman was concerned with Samantha's mental stability. She was the only one who had seen one of these things and still been somewhat coherent. Drusilla had also managed to put the images of swirling fog and black smoke from her vision with Darven into a semblance of understanding. The smoke had been the creatures. They had killed him for betraying them, although the whereabouts of his physical body were still unknown, they were likely somewhere onboard the *Odyssey*.

The crew were seemingly at the mercy of an incredibly intelligent and sentient species. The evidence was there for all to see. They had lured the Darla to the edge of the

Expanse, invaded their minds, and forced them to lure others to their home. And if they failed, they were destroyed as well. The real sign that they had intentions was in their deliberate luring of the *Odyssey* back to their space. It had of course been here before under the command of Admiral Harry Ransome. But he had escaped, and clearly these creatures were not about to let the humans go so easily.

Drusilla stood from her chair, picked up a medical scanner, and headed towards Matteo to take her latest set of readings. However, half way there, a blinding pain tore through her head, and she collapsed to the floor, the scanner smashing as it hit the deck. She rolled uncontrollably, screaming as the pain sparked from temple to temple. Roman rushed down beside her, but her legs met him square in the chest and with some incredible force managed to launch him backwards through the air, slamming against the opposite wall. Her eyes flew open, but they were no longer their usual shade of icy blue. *They were fiery red.*

Her screams slowly began to change from agony and anguish and morphed slowly, but clearly into hysterical laughter. Drusilla's face changed too. She began to smile, and her lips spread wide to reveal a gleaming tooth-filled grimace. The voice was not her own, but it was extremely clear, as she stood up and glared at Roman as he dragged himself back to his feet.

"Hahaha. You pathetic little creatures. You will not stop the feast. We will devour you all, as we did your ancestors. We will tear your minds apart before we tear your flesh from the bones."

Everybody was now backed up against the nearest wall, except Roman, who despite being terrified, began to move towards Drusilla, hand out in front of him.

"Dru, it's me. I know that's not you, but you have to fight

them. They were in my head too, and I know what it's like. You have to push them out. You have the power."

But Drusilla continued to laugh heartily, and spat through her words.

"She cannot help you, human. Like her ancestor failed to stop us devouring his crew, she will fail to stop us devouring yours. She even sped up the process for us."

Drusilla's eyes flashed for a moment, and Roman swore he saw the glacier blue of her eyes trying to break through the fire within them, and he saw sadness. But it lasted only a moment. Drusilla licked her lips, and then slowly ran her tongue along her teeth as she started to move toward Noah, who was the nearest person to her.

"Dru, hey, it's okay. It's me, Noah. Don't listen to these things, you can fight this!"

Noah started to move along the wall towards Roman, who in turn tried to move towards Noah. Drusilla grabbed hold of Roman's combat vest and threw him again, this time in the opposite direction, and he landed just shy of Matteo, landing in a heap at Samantha's feet. As Noah tried to make a break for it, she slammed a fist into his side, and there was no mistaking the sound of several ribs breaking upon impact. Noah crumpled to the floor, gasping for air, but she did not stop. She *couldn't* stop. They wouldn't let her. She kept pummelling Noah, harder and harder. Each bone that broke seemed to encourage her tormentors to go further. Noah's blood coated her fists, and he had long stopped moving, his head merely a mess of brain matter and tenderised flesh on the floor. Samantha was in the corner of the room screaming, and Roman was trying to drag himself along the floor. Blow after blow continued, Drusilla's face a picture of pure ecstasy, blood showering her face, trickling down it like beads of sweat. Her clothes were sodden with it, and yet they forced her to keep going.

Roman threw everything he had into the punch. The overwhelming desire he had to keep Drusilla safe had to have been pushed to the side. He had watched the woman he loved turn his best friend into nothing but a mound of bloodied pulp. One way or another, he had to stop her. Her jawbone took the brunt of the strike, but her nose shifted slightly as well, and as she collapsed down beside Noah's body, the fire slowly vanished from her eyes, and as they closed, they returned to their usual blue.

Roman glanced briefly over at Noah, his chest aching with the need to scream, but he shoved it back down. Not now. Not now. They will reach the other side of the Expanse. And when they did, he was going to make these bastards pay.

TWENTY FIVE

THE BLANKET WAS NOWHERE NEAR BIG ENOUGH TO COVER
Noah's remains. There was no way it could be called a body
any longer. The simply horrific violence that had taken place
could not even begin to be imagined by anyone outside of the
four walls of engineering. It had been a week since Drusilla
had been possessed by the creatures outside and murdered
one of her dearest friends. The entire time that had passed
since, she had remained mute, tucked up in the corner, staring
at the sheet and the two legs and mangled hands that
protruded from beneath it. The scenes kept running over and
over again in front of her eyes. She was torturing herself. But
in truth, it also acted as a defence mechanism to keep the
creatures out of her mind. By replaying the scene over and
over, she was preventing there being any gaps in
concentration as she could keep control. Her doors had not
worked, and it had cost them dearly. And worse of all, the
other three now knew this was not the first time she had fallen
victim to this invasion of the mind.

Samantha had said next to nothing. She too had the image
of Noah's lifeless and virtually gelatinous remains burned into

the back of her skull. She had only really spoken to excuse herself to use the facilities, or to check on the flight plan. Matteo, by this point was now up and alert. He had not been conscious during the attack on Noah, and his remains were one of the first things he saw. Rather depressingly, his witness to Carlos' dismembering had strengthened his resolve upon seeing Noah's beaten face for the first time. A quality he sorely wished he had not developed.

As for Roman, he had spent his time trying to scan the inside of the Expanse to look for some kind of indication of what they faced. When the sensors continued to come back with nothing, he had started to search for a way to cross the void of space faster. The engines were out, as confirmed by Matteo as he relayed the story of tearing out vital cables to rescue Carlos. A rescue that had ultimately been in vain, but had also served to cripple them further. Matteo was now convinced that had been their plan all along. Slow them down. Remove any prospect of escape, and simply wait for them to run out of momentum, or venture out into the ship where they would be completely at the creatures' mercy.

"Holy shit."

The words took them all by surprise, as Roman conveyed them with such emotion, it snapped them all out of their trances. It was the first words not uttered in routine formality in a week.

"Ho-ly shit!"

The extra enunciation captured Samantha's attention so greatly that she rushed to his side, pushing past Drusilla without even acknowledging her. A gesture which caused her to shrink back to where she had started.

"What? What is it?" Samantha asked eagerly.

"There's something out there."

Those four words sent a chill down everyone's spine,

including Roman's as he said them. He'd seen the data for himself, and cross run the scans five times to be sure, but somehow uttering them made them more real.

"What? How can that be? This is meant to be empty space!"

Samantha didn't want to get ahead of herself, but couldn't help the slow and gradual rise of something akin to hope within her.

"So what is it?" asked Matteo, getting up from the relocated medical bed.

Roman pointed to the screen, and tapped the glass enthusiastically.

"No way."

"Holy shit."

Roman nodded and couldn't stop a smile appearing in the corner of his mouth.

"Yup. It's a planet."

TWENTY-SIX

"So, LET ME GET THIS STRAIGHT. YOU WANT US TO LEAVE engineering. The place where we have been safe for ten days now, and wander the hallways?"

Samantha's tone was not an encouraging one, and Roman couldn't help but glance down at Noah's remains and thinking this room had turned out to not be entirely safe after all. But the facts were facts.

"Sam, we're nearly out of food, we used all the med supplies treating Matteo, and this mystery planet is still six days away with no means to accelerate the journey. What do you suggest we do?"

Samantha opened her mouth to immediately deliver a comeback, but stopped short when she realised she didn't have one.

"I'll go."

Drusilla's choked words barely registered with Samantha. In fact, the pilot didn't even turn round to acknowledge them. She knew that Drusilla had not been responsible for Noah's death, and that her body was merely a vessel for the demons that taunted them from inside their own ship. But she couldn't forgive her for not telling them that this had happened before, and she'd been used to kill both Dante and Aliah.

"No."

Roman's voice was authoritative and decisive.

"I'm the logical choice," Drusilla protested. "These fuckers can use me to get to EVERYBODY I care about. I... I did this!"

She was pointing to Noah, her finger trembling as she fought back tears.

"They used me to kill my friends, and I'll be damned if it's all for nothing!"

Again, unwavering in his decision, his hands crossed tightly against his chest, Roman replied, "No."

"I mean, if you wanna be technical, I'm the obvious choice."

Matteo moved out of one of the shadows along the far wall, checking over a disruptor with his remaining hand. "I'm the most expendable."

Roman's voice tore through the debate, so there was no mistake in what he was about to say.

"NONE OF YOU ARE FUCKING EXPENDABLE!" He turned to Matteo. "You could have no legs, and half a stomach hanging out and I wouldn't send you out there, so don't think a missing hand makes you disposable!" Drusilla was next in his sights. "And you, Dru, are more valuable with us, here. I need you to work on something while I'm gone."

Drusilla span around and punched the wall, hard. The skin was still bruised and broken from beating Noah to death, and the pain caused her to cradle her hands.

"I can't keep them out, Roman. I've tried! Even now, I can feel them peeling away at the inside of my head! They're toying with me!"

Roman lowered his arms and walked towards her. He took her face in his hands, leaned close and looked deep into her eyes.

"I don't want you to focus on stopping them from entering your mind... I want you to focus on entering theirs."

TWENTY-SEVEN

3RD DECEMBER 2332

THE SHINE ON THE GLOSSY WALLS GLINTED IN THE sparkle of the overhead lighting, momentarily blinding Admiral Harry Ransome. But he couldn't help but smile. This was it. Everything he had worked for, everything he had fought for was about to come to fruition. In less than twenty-four hours, he was going to lead Earth's greatest minds out into the unknown, searching for new homes, and new species. He was determined in his resolve, and would ensure humanity survived, whatever the cost.

"You're in your peacock mode, Harry."

The newly minted Admiral chuckled as the last couple of spots faded from his vision, and he lay his eyes upon the most beautiful woman he had ever known. The President of Earth had been the one who gave Harry Ransome the go ahead to develop the *Utopia* project and her faith in him had never wavered, even when there had been minor setbacks. Many years before, they had fought together on both Mars and Jupiter, emerging victorious.

"She's beautiful, ain't she?" he replied, running his left palm along one of the currently offline consoles in what would become his quarters. The very first room behind the bridge, keeping him close to the action, but giving him his own private space. The architects of the *Odyssey* had offered to create an office, or ready room for him, directly linked to the bridge, but he declined. An office would have made it feel too much like he was at work. He wanted to feel like he was on an ocean liner, and retire to his cabin every night after watching the stars sail by.

"She should be. This ship is the most advanced of the fleet, the largest, and cost the most to build. I'd better see some return on my investment, Ransome."

Although her words were authoritative, they were spoken through a wide smile. They both spent an eternity locked in the moment. Harry was still so in awe of his new ship, but also acutely aware that this was likely the last time he would see the beautiful creature before him. He glanced down at his glistening black boots, and spoke to the floor. He had never been one for direct eye contact at an awkward moment.

"Look, I don't know what we're going to find out there. I don't know the dangers we are going to come up against, and I can't guarantee we're even gonna make it back. So I just wanted you to know..."

Harry stopped speaking instantly. As his eyes had fixed on the floor, he had seen the appearance of a dress. He slowly slid his gaze upwards, and when it returned to the woman in front of him, he saw that she was now completely naked. Any speech he was about to make was now gone entirely from his mind. Harry's eyes explored every inch of her body, and moments later, words weren't needed. The two of them embraced and spent what would be their last night together, simply *being* together.

Harry couldn't sleep. Despite the evening's activities, slumber was a stranger to him. He had been staring at the carpeted ceiling in his quarters for so long now, that he had noticed a few loose threads and had made a mental note to have those repaired. Occasionally, he would glance over at the President, who was still comfortably dozing, the sheets wrapped loosely around her body. Every so often, she would smile, and hug her pillow tighter to her face, and Harry hoped she was dreaming of him.

But he was afraid. Not of the mission itself, or travelling across the galaxy at faster than light speeds. He was afraid of being discovered. It had been sixteen years since a very young Harry Ransome had lied about his age to enlist in the first war between Earth and Mars. He'd been so eager that he had never questioned his orders, and slaughtered the human rebels without hesitation. When the word was sent that Jupiter's colonists had also chosen to fight against their home planet, he had been the first to sign up with his new officer's rank. It had almost been too easy. Those settled on Jupiter still had not fully adjusted to their terraformed climate, which robbed them of any potential home advantage. They were even easier to cut down than the Mars detachment.

But it wasn't these two wars he was afraid of coming back to bite him. It was the two that followed them.

Eight years prior, the third war in a decade was declared, this time against a previously undetected species native to Mars. They were called the Legatans. They'd been driven underground by the invading humans over a decade ago, but were now re-emerging to claim back their planet. By this point he had become a fully fledged Captain, and was not simply commanding units of men and women, but the entire human forces. After almost eighteen months of fighting, the Legatans surrendered, and both they and Ransome signed a peace treaty. It was broadcast to every human across the Sol System no matter where they were, and everyone had cheered Captain Harry Ransome. He was declared a hero to humanity, and lauded as such. And that was when he met the current President of Earth.

She was not in her prestigious role at that time, and arrived on Mars not long after the treaty had been signed. Harry was captivated by her immediately. He had a wife and children back on Earth, but this woman worked her way into his mind, and he simply couldn't resist her. The very first night they met, they slept together. The feeling was so euphoric that he almost became addicted to her presence. She spoke of how dangerous the Legatans had been, and the threat they continued to pose. Harry made the argument that the job was done, but she insisted they were still a danger to Earth, and she demanded something be done about them to ensure nothing would harm humanity ever again.

After just one night together, Harry Ransome, commanding the human forces against the Legatans, ordered that each and every one of the native species be terminated immediately. He could not understand at the time, why he felt so compelled to do so, but he felt the whole time as if the future President's hand was on his shoulder, guiding him through his choices and decisions. The massacre was never reported of course, and Ransome continued to be praised as a hero, which only increased a hundred fold when he led his final foray into battle against the also previously undetected native species of Jupiter.

Only eight months separated the third and fourth wars of the Sol System, and in that entire time, Harry Ransome had been seeing this mystery woman every time he was away from home. He had distanced himself from his own family, his children no longer called him father, but instead referred to him as Captain, and he found any excuse he could to get away from them. But in the arms of his lover, he found solace, and comfort. His mind would ease into a place he could not find without her guidance, and infatuation had turned into dependency.

The name of Jupiter's indigenous species was the Darla.

During the terraforming exercise begun by humanity, they had been forced to leave the planet and seek refuge on two of the planet's four moons. Humans had used Io and Ganymede for refuelling stations, and personnel transfers, and so the Darla chose to hide on Europa and Callisto. This time, the future president took a keen interest in the war, enlisting under the supervision of Captain Ransome, but the reality was she was the one in control. She convinced him to make her his second in command. She was capable of creating and giving out orders, and if they required higher authorisation, she would simply work her magic and he would approve them.

She wanted the Darla dead. All of them. No exceptions. She gave no reasoning, and no quarter. Between the two of them alone, she and Harry spilled the blood of almost six thousand Darla civilians.

And that was when the mission parameters changed.

Over a hundred Darla evacuee vessels made it away from Jupiter, and with the Earth vessels not yet ready, the *Utopia* concept only just being put onto paper, they were powerless to stop them. The future President returned to Earth, where she became the *current* President of Earth, and scheduled a private meeting with Captain Ransome.

"I will approve your plans for humanity, if you promise me one thing."

"Anything my love."

"Hunt. Down. The. Darla."

And now, here he was. Now Admiral Ransome, about to lead humanity on an expedition into space, not to explore, but as glorified bounty hunters. And for the first time, his mind felt like his own, and the discomfort surged throughout his body. He let out a long and heavy sigh, and the President shifted next to him.

"Harry? Are you okay?" she said groggily as she pushed herself up onto her elbow and turned to face him.

But he wasn't distracted this time at the sight of her body, the sheets falling away from her as she moved. He had never felt clearer in all the time they had known each other.

"I can't do this," he said softly. "I can't sacrifice humanity to hunt down some refugees. It's not right."

Fury began to flare on the President's face, as she raised herself to a fully seated position. Harry felt the energy surging between the two of them and for the first time, he was not enamoured by it. He was afraid of it.

"Harry Ransome. You will listen to me very, very carefully. You will continue as I instructed, and you will not deviate from the plan. Is that understood?"

Her eyes burned into his own. But the burn was not that of fire, but of *ice*. The glacier-like quality of those eyes had always mesmerised him, and he was powerless to tear himself away from them. Even the strands of her long, blue hair falling over them could not break the effect. He felt this woman almost reach into his mind, and squeeze until he submitted to her, entirely. And just like that, the brief and fleeting feel of independence was gone from Harry, and he became almost possessed once more.

"Yes, Drusilla. I understand."

TWENTY-EIGHT

PRESENT DAY

IN TRUTH, BOTH ROMAN AND SAMANTHA WERE GLAD TO be out of engineering, although they were only in the adjoining storage room. Matteo and Drusilla were still sealed in main engineering, but these two felt it important to relocate Noah's remains. Not to put too fine a point to it, but a body in that state after over a week, was beginning to *smell*. In the storage room, were airtight containers, similar to those from the cargo bay, but significantly larger. They needed to house the likes of engine coils and probes. This made them the ideal length to store a human body in and prevent further decay. It had of course been a risk, as the alien creatures could have attacked them at any moment, but with Drusilla preparing for an entirely unprecedented form of attack, he wanted to give her as much space as possible. Samantha being armed with not one, but five disruptors didn't hurt either. As they lowered Noah into the container and closed the lid, they both paid their respects to their fallen comrade, and slumped down onto a neighbouring container, housing stem bolts.

"You think we can trust her?"

Samantha's question was poised delicately, but it had already circled Roman's mind a hundred times or more since her possession. Drusilla now felt a long way away from the woman he knew. Her personality had become more fragile and fragmented, her emotions more unstable, and now she had shrunk back into herself. He couldn't put his finger on it, but something had changed in her.

"Honestly? I have no idea."

His reply caught Samantha a little off guard. She had expected him to be fully loyal to Drusilla, and believed them to now be a couple. It brought her some relief, and her shoulders began to relax a little.

"Wow, I didn't expect that," she said.

"What?"

"You not leaping to the defence of your blue haired vixen there."

Roman scoffed.

"She's not mine, Sam. I'm not even sure she's her anymore."

"What do you mean?"

Roman ran both hands over his face, as if trying to clear an obstruction from his eyes.

"She jumped me, back on Azanti Prime. Came out of nowhere. I went to shower, and the next minute she was there, and she..."

"Yeah, I got it. We all saw you know? It wasn't exactly subtle. Some of us got quite jealous."

Roman raised one eyebrow and turned his head toward her. She held up her hands and stopped him before he could make a sarcastic comment.

"Hey, I said jealous, not infatuated!"

"Just gonna file that away under 'potential blackmail' for future reference."

The two of them shared a brief giggle, which drowned out the slight sound of a pointed tail just catching the edge of the doorway. Samantha continued.

"So what's so bad about that? Hunter had been gone for a while at that point, and you two were always close. I thought it's what you wanted."

Roman shook his head, as a second tail snaked it's way above them, in the darkness.

"It didn't feel right. It didn't feel like *her*. I felt like she was trying to control the situation, and then afterwards, when the possibility of finding the *Odyssey* reached touching distance, she pushed me to the back burner."

"But you've always wanted to find this ship, I mean you were borderline obsessed about it."

Roman shook his head again.

"That's just it, Sam. I don't give a shit about this ship. It's literally a pay check for me. I've never wanted to find this, because as far as I was concerned, humanity is all but gone and there's no point in pining after relics or dead ancestors."

Samantha stood up, and her eyes caught movement in the corner of the room, against the ceiling. She quickly glanced at Roman, but he was already aware that they were being watched, and simply nodded to continue talking.

"But it was you who said we had to go and track their engine trail. Then you decided we would rebuild the *Belle Vue* and track any energy signals to try and find this ship. It consumed you entirely!"

Roman gradually stood up and walked towards her, his hand clenching the handle of his own disruptor.

"That's the thing, Sam. That wasn't *me*."

A gust of wind engulfed them both as a tail whipped through the air, getting so close to Roman, it sliced a lock of his hair, which then floated to the ground. But they had been prepared for this. Both of them dropped to the ground, spun to face the creatures, and unloaded their full power cell from all six weapons they were carrying between them. High pitched shrieks of pain shrouded the room, and both Roman and Samantha had to resist the urge to cover their ears. One of the creatures attempted to whip its tail in Samantha's direction, but Roman fired a shot into its path, and the tip of it was cut clean from the rest. As it thrashed in pain, and the cries became almost excruciating, the creature's blood began to spray the room like a fire hose. But they didn't stop firing, until all but one of the disruptor power cells was depleted, and they heard two distinct thuds in the dim glow of the emergency lights.

The only sound in the room was now that of Samantha and Roman's heightened breathing. The rush of monster blood from the first creature's tail had stopped, and the tip lay just beyond Roman's feet. Checking to make sure Samantha still had her remaining disruptor aimed into the darkness, he leaned forward and picked up the tip of the tail between his fingers. Immediately, the sheer sharpness of the thing sliced into his thumb and forefinger. He winced and dropped it back to the floor.

And then he saw it.

The blood from the creature which had been on the severed tail, had mixed with his own, and as he watched on, eyes wide and unable to break away, the cuts to his finger and thumb began to *heal*.

"What in the name of all that's holy?" he blurted out.

"What's wrong?" Samantha asked, but she answered her own question when she approached him and just caught the end of the healing process.

"Woah."

"Yeah."

For a moment or two, Roman feared he may start to mutate or burn from the inside, like in all of those old sci-fi movies he'd seen as a kid. But no. He was perfectly normal, and more than that, he was able to note that only the affected wound had been healed. Others he had sustained over the last eleven days were very much still present.

"Uh, Roman?"

He was still examining his hand.

"Yeah, Sam?"

"If you're healing from a drop of their blood, and they're full of it..."

Roman was already turning around and dragging Samantha toward the door before the sound of the previously dead creatures rising began. A low but loud growl came from the far corner, as sure enough, they began to heal. Samantha leaped through the door, but Roman stopped, turned quickly, and pulled a thick glove from his waistband. Darting forward, he wrapped the tip of tail within it, and sprinted back for the doorway.

Slamming the mechanism with his hand as hard as he could, the doors slammed shut just as one of the creatures leapt into the light. The image of the monster fully revealed burned itself into Roman's eyes, and he saw it long after the door had closed.

TWENTY-NINE

THEY WERE GETTING SMARTER. NOT THAT THESE THINGS had ever been stupid. Far from it. They were meticulous hunters. But their minds were something completely different. Drusilla usually reached out to someone in order to feel their emotions, or manipulate their feelings in order to calm them. She had often taken anger from Roman, and replaced it with peace. But despite three hours of trying, she couldn't detect these things let alone infiltrate one's mind. Even after Samantha and Roman had flown around the corner having just escaped from two of them. She even knew where they were, and pressed her hand against the connecting wall, trying to feel them somehow. But nothing happened. The ship seemed as empty as the Expanse. Of course that had proven deceptive, and that notion had given her the strength to continue searching for them.

Before the attack, Roman had managed to find a small selection of snacks in the storage room, and some coffee pods, albeit with no water. They decided after their narrow escape that they could postpone their suicide mission of hunting for more supplies one more day and live on the century old chocolate, which to its credit, was actually not half bad.

Whilst the other two had been away, Drusilla had noticed Matteo acting strangely. He would be sat on his medical bed one minute, reading a schematic from the nearby screens, and then the next, he would be talking to himself. Most of the words went under the range of her hearing, but just a few minutes before Roman and Samantha had returned, she had definitively heard him utter the words 'they regenerate.'

It was happening again. She could almost see the invisible rope connecting her to Matteo's head. She had no control of why this was happening, but she had noticed things long before they were trapped here. She would suddenly feel a chill under her skin, like a cold fire burning, and then Roman, or sometimes Hunter when he was alive, would shift moods suddenly and unexpectedly. She had started to wonder if whatever memories she could not find, were linked to her abilities and that for whatever reason they were now coming to the fore. The guilt of what happened with Dante and Aliah had almost torn her apart. But Noah was like a brother to her. That had truly broken her. Now she couldn't even find who she was now, let alone whoever she used to be.

A hand landed gently on her shoulder, and Drusilla turned expecting to see Roman, but instead found Matteo. A brief smile flickered away from her face as he sat down next to her. Over her shoulder, she could see Roman conversing with Samantha, describing the creature in all its grotesque delight. She felt something shoot through her entire core that she had never felt before. *Jealousy*. Matteo attempted to capture her attention.

"Hey, so I need to ask you... how do you do that?"

"Do what?" she asked, genuinely unsure of what he meant.

"You know, show me things."

Drusilla was confused. To her knowledge she had been entirely focussed on attempting to enter the mind of a monster.

"What are you talking about?" she retorted.

"One minute I'm evaluating the engine designs, and then I see you in my mind, and you're guiding me through that wall."

Matteo pointed at the connecting wall which had earlier separated them from the creatures. He continued.

"And then you pointed at one of those... those things, and spoke to me."

Drusilla's attention had been captured. She had no memory of any of this.

"What did I say?" she asked.

"They regenerate."

Drusilla's spine shivered and her blood turned to ice. How was this possible? She had no idea that the creatures had this ability. Frankly, they had been hard enough to keep away from as it was, before they discovered they were nigh on unkillable.

"Matteo, I have no idea what you're talking about, but I don't remember any of this. I didn't even know that the Raxar even had that ability."

It was Matteo's turn to have his blood run cold.

"How do you know their name?" he asked, backing away cautiously. The fear was etched on his face, and he was not alone. Both Roman and Samantha had heard what was said. The former moved closer, the others moving away.

"Dru, how do you know what they're called?" Roman spoke with only one emotion. Anger. Somehow, she had known their name all this time. But how. And why?

"I- I don't.... I don't know."

185

Drusilla's voice was a pleading one, and tears began to form at the edge of her eyes. She was dredging through her memory trying to find any source for the name which had escaped her lips. She couldn't find one. There was no memory attached to the name Raxar. But the terrifying thing to her, was the fact that despite this, it felt *familiar*.

"That name didn't just pop up by accident. Raxar. That's not a random word you pluck out of the goddamn air. Now tell me how you know them!"

"I DON'T FUCKING KNOW ROMAN!"

Drusilla collapsed on a heap in the floor, lost in uncontrollable sobs. Nobody approached her. Roman actually chose to back away towards the others, but he didn't break his gaze. He had come back from next door with Samantha's question still rolling around in his mind.

You think we can trust her?

Roman now knew the answer to that question, despite his hate surrounding the admission of it.

The answer, was no.

THIRTY

THE GLOW OF THE RED BEACONS SHINING AGAINST THEIR thick, black armoured skin was a sickening sight to behold. Now their true appearance had been revealed to them, the Raxar weren't even bothering to hide anymore. They knew they were stronger, faster, and more deadly. Even though he had seen them once before, Roman had not allowed for the influence he felt standing in their presence. But needs must, and their short-lived chocolate bounty was now gone. A supply run had to be made, but Roman knew he'd be sliced in half before he even got to the secondary cargo bay which was located one deck below them.

Drusilla had been unable to tell him anything more about the Raxar, where they came from, what they wanted besides to feed on human flesh or even how she knew their name. Reluctantly, he and the others had decided to isolate her in the adjacent storage room in which he and Samantha had nearly been killed. It screamed at him from within his brain that he was doing the wrong thing, but he knew that despite her continued protests of innocence, she knew things somehow about the creatures hunting them. And rather than giving them an advantage, it put them in mortal danger.

What he wasn't expecting, was this. When he opened the door to engineering, he immediately saw three of the Raxar hunched half way up the wall directly opposite. They leered there, approximately eight feet in height, and easily five feet across from shoulder to shoulder. Their skin was black, and shining, not with a viscous substance, but with a hard shell finish similar to a beetle. In terms of anatomy, they looked resembled a scorpion. The long and pointed tails, whipping around behind them during battle, were now planted against the white gloss walls of the *Odyssey's* corridor. Their head was elongated, and appeared to simply be a skull. The only defining feature of their faces were the long and narrow red eyes which burned and glowed with fire, and their enormous pointed teeth, slightly yellowed, razor sharp, and slick with thick drool.

And the unexpected part? When he saw them, Roman called out their name.

"You are Raxar."

One looked towards the others, tilting its head as if in thought. When it returned its gaze to Roman, it leapt forward and landed on the floor, extending its body fully upright, almost brushing the ceiling. A low growl emanated from its throat. And then it spoke.

"You are correct."

The voice was of the creature, but it did not come from the Raxar. The words came from Drusilla's mouth. Roman moved away from her, but kept his eyes on the Raxar at all times. Drusilla's eyes were now that fiery red they had been when she killed Noah, but her voice bore no expression. This time they were using her as a mouthpiece only. Therefore, Roman directed his questions to the Raxar directly.

"How does Dru know your name?" he asked, trying to keep any quivers out of it and failing. Drusilla's mouth responded.

"We have encountered her before. Many years ago. She knows us, but does not know herself."

Something told Roman, he wasn't going to like the next answer.

"How many years ago?"

Another low growl came from the lead Raxar's mouth, and Roman watched as it's mouth spread wider as if inciting a smile of some sort. Drusilla's mouth mimicked the action and Roman was immediately covered in goosebumps.

"Almost two centuries ago."

Roman didn't realise he had been holding in a breath until he let it out. Then he took another one. And another one. Each quicker than the last. Drusilla was over two hundred years old. Either she didn't know that, or she was a damn good liar.

"What do you want with us? Why do you want *us* here?"

Roman was screaming at the Raxar now, fuelled by fear, hatred and betrayal. This seemed to excite the creatures, and all three of them now donned the sickening grin. Drusilla turned slowly towards him, her grin now as wide as her face would allow.

"Because we like the taste of your flesh."

It all happened so quickly, had it not been for Samantha, Roman would have been decapitated there and then. The lead Raxar had used Drusilla to distract him long enough that he had leaned forward and opened its mouth beyond its limits. The sound of bones cracking in its jaw are what alerted Samantha, who pulled Roman away just as the mouth clamped down on where his head had been just milliseconds before. Drusilla, now freed from her controllers, slumped forward to her knees. The lead Raxar swept an arm through the air, and the spines on the back of its arm sliced through a staggering Matteo's back, and he fell forwards, his face smashing into the hard floor, his nose exploding with blood on contact.

"DON'T LET THEM TOUCH YOU!"

Roman's voice rang out in the corridor, but with every flash of red emergency lighting, the Raxar had moved another metre towards them. They ducked and dodged the flailing razor sharp limbs more by luck than anything else, and desperately tried to reach Matteo who was still on the ground attempting to drag himself forward. But even that effort soon became futile. An enormous clawed foot slammed down into Matteo's back, and through some kind of muscle clench, the talons on the end of each toe extended and then slammed down piercing Matteo's skin. He screamed until it felt as though his lungs were going to burst. The Raxar who had spoken to them was now stood blocking the door to engineering. They had no choice. They had to run for it. Samantha pulled a maintenance hatch off the wall, and ducked inside. Good, too small for one of those things.

"IN HERE!" she shouted trying to be heard over Matteo's dying screams.

Roman grabbed Drusilla, and threw her into the tunnel, Samantha following after her, still not happy even in these circumstances, to have her out of sight. Roman hovered, one foot inside the hatch, and one out. As he watched, all three Raxar amassed around Matteo. The first brought its teeth down on his left leg, and with one small movement, tore the entire limb free without effort. Matteo's screams were now beyond him, and he began to gurgle speech through his own blood.

"Help... me!"

A second Raxar tore off Matteo's right arm at the shoulder, whilst the third tore a chunk of flesh from between his shoulder blades.

Roman's view began to blur between tears. There was only one thing he could do to help his friend. He clutched his disruptor in his hand. Enough charge left for one shot. He looked up at his friend, as Matteo's blood sprayed up the corridor walls from another torn limb, this time his left arm.

"I'm sorry."

As soon as he spoke the words, Roman fired his last shot between Matteo's dying eyes, and instantly his friend was at rest. Matteo would be spared anymore pain. The entire ship rocked with the screams of anger from the three Raxar. Matteo was dead, and they no longer had live flesh to feed from. There were no hysterical impulses, accelerated heartbeats to pump the blood round as they feasted. They were *furious*.

"Oh fuck."

When Roman realised, he leapt into the hatch and slammed the panel back into place. Unlike their previous encounters, the Raxar began pounding at the hatch door panel, dents appearing in it with each strike. Samantha, Drusilla and now Roman crawled their way through the tunnels as fast as their limbs would take them. The hammering on the hatch continued, before the razor pointed tip of a tail pierced the metal. The Raxar had been the puppeteers up until now, toying with the crew, manipulating their actions, sabotaging their ship, simply to make their hunt more exciting. But now they had been denied a fresh kill.

And now, they were *angry*.

THIRTY-ONE

THE SOUND COMFORT OF SLEEP NEVER DID COME TO Roman. He and the others had gone to great lengths to seal themselves inside a second maintenance tunnel they had found, deeper into the ship. It was a risk, because now they were a good forty minutes crawl away from the nearest open space, but he also knew the Raxar would not be able to enter this space. They were far too big. An excellent predator in the open, or striking from the shadows, but in a confined space, they were neutered.

As Roman slumped against one of the walls, Samantha began to stir. She had fallen asleep purely due to exhaustion. She had been running on so much adrenaline and fear, that once she was certain they would be safe in this location, she more or less passed out. She propped herself up, but a thin imprint of the floor grating was visible on her face. The sight made Roman smile.

"What?"

"You look like you slept on a cheese grater."

She felt her face, and ran her fingertips over the bumps. After a moment, she snorted herself. That proceeded to wake

Drusilla, who too had fallen asleep simply from exhaustion, but much further down the corridor than the others. The distance was both required and demanded by their circumstances. They didn't trust her, and quite frankly, she didn't trust herself.

This was not their first night in the tunnels. This was their *fourth*. Roman had decided to let the others sleep. They needed to be refreshed and as ready as possible to take on what lay ahead. Somehow, they had to get themselves to that planet. But their flight course, locked in by Samantha herself, didn't even know the planet was there. If they didn't intervene, then in twenty-four hours, they would go happily sailing by. Roman suspected it wouldn't take that long for the Raxar to find a way to them, and he suspected that way would be Drusilla.

There were two problems with that, however. Problem number one, was that the bridge was gone and the decks below and surrounding it had no breathable air. Problem number two, was that the Raxar now controlled engineering, and although they would not be able to physically alter the course or any of the controls of the *Odyssey* (lacking normal sized limbs), it did prevent Roman and the others from doing so themselves. That meant one thing, but he wasn't ready to tell them that yet.

"Dru?" he called out. "You okay?"

Drusilla turned and gave him a weak smile, and a gentle nod. She was physically fine, refreshed from sleep, and had built up some energy reserves. But mentally, she was as fractured as a sheet of broken ice. During her four days of sleep and rest, her mind had flashed images of things she didn't recognise and yet at the same time felt familiar. How could such a contradiction exist? She saw the *Odyssey* newly launched, brief memories of various battlefields. The other memories however, disturbed her greatly. She saw Harry Ransome and herself in bed together. It was not the same image each time, but varying ones, in various locations, at various times. She knew that it was impossible to have those memories, those feelings. She was only in her mid-thirties, and Harry Ransome had been dead over a century, at least. But there they were. Flicking behind her eyes like a picture book. She wondered if she should talk to Roman, but she didn't think he could help her, and probably wouldn't believe her. She still couldn't explain the Raxar name coming from her lips, and had no idea what they had meant by saying they had met before. But hour by hour, her mental stability was in freefall, and her major worry now, was if she reached true breaking point, would she simply be inviting the Raxar into her mind. If that happened, it would be an empty ship reaching the Horizon.

Samantha was attempting to remove her shirt further down the corridor, but the laceration she had received to her right arm in the scramble to escape four days earlier, combined with the low ceiling meant the most mundane task was proving frustrating. The dressing was now in need of changing, but in anger, she tore the collar of her shirt and cried out in frustration.

"Let me help with that."

Roman's voice made her jump slightly, as she had not noticed him approach. She kept her back turned to him for privacy, but she had to admit, she couldn't treat her arm without help, and she damn sure wasn't letting Drusilla anywhere near her. Roman helped her carefully lift her shirt over her head, keeping her arms at a slight angle to match the bend in the tunnel design, and then handed it back to her so she could cover herself.

"You know that's a pretty deep one," he said examining the wound.

"Yeah well, I didn't exactly have a hospital to stroll to, so I got on with it."

Samantha immediately regretted being short with her boss. In truth, she was trying to treat the wound in an effort to take her mind away from Matteo. Every time she thought about why they had spent four days and nights in a glorified air vent, she saw his tortured face, and the limbs being torn away from his body. One night she had dreamt that every time a leg or arm was torn away, snakes came spilling out of the joints and slithered their way toward her, drowning her in a serpentine wave. This was the reason behind the smaller cut to her forehead, and its surrounding bruise.

"Sorry," she whispered to him. "It's just a lot, you know?"

Roman nodded, then realised she couldn't see him.

"Yeah, I get it. But if it helps you can blame me."

She turned her head.

"Why would I blame you?" she asked, a quizzical look on her face.

"I was the one who brought us here. It's on me."

Samantha's quizzical look turned to anger, but her eyes bore sympathy.

"This is not your fault Roman. You set a course here under the influence of some alien presence, whose body, by the way, we still haven't found. You, as yourself, the real you? You didn't do this."

Roman reached into a small pouch in his vest and pulled out a small sewing kit. Inside, he found a very thin needle and bundle of black thread. Samantha saw it, and winced automatically. She knew what was coming. She's had to have field treatment before.

"If I hadn't been so determined to find this fucking ship,

maybe everyone would still be alive. That was long before Darven took control of my mind."

Samantha batted away the sewing kit, and grabbed his face with both hands.

"You are not responsible for this, Roman. We all followed you, we knew what we were doing, and we all wanted this prize. Money, fame, doesn't matter why. But we all knew what we were getting ourselves into, and that's on us. Not you."

Roman looked into her eyes, and he knew that she was telling the truth. He still blamed himself, and always would, whatever anybody said to him. It was part of the burden of being a leader. But some of the weight lifted off him in that moment, and he felt closer to Samantha than he'd every considered. In her rush to comfort him, Samantha had allowed her shirt to fall to the ground, and did not realise, until a harsh cough came from behind him. Drusilla did not look impressed, and gestured to Samantha's now entirely visible breasts.

"Oh shit," she said, and scrambled to cover herself back up. Roman gave Drusilla a very stern look, and in the interests of moving on, put away the sewing kit, and instead replaced the bandage with a new one. Drusilla had no right to question any conversation or indeed situation. She had burned her bridges with them, and it was now simply a matter of keeping her safe so he could find out what the hell she knew.

"So what now?" she asked curtly, not taking her eyes off Samantha as she continued to struggle to replace her shirt.

"We need to get to a control access point, or we aren't going to make it to the planet."

Drusilla had no idea where any of these were beyond the obvious two. The bridge and engineering. And yet...

"Deck One."

Roman and Samantha both looked at her stunned, even

though it should have come to no surprise tat Drusilla was somehow still harbouring knowledge of unknown quantities.

"What did you say?" she asked.

"Deck One. There's an override console linked to the Captain's Quarters in case of emergencies. His quarters are on Deck One, behind the bridge. Or where the bridge used to be."

Drusilla had no idea how she knew this, beyond a faint memory of being in that very room, which again was impossible. But she was done trying to explain what she didn't know, and made this fact very clear to the others.

"Look, I don't know how the fuck I know any of this, and I can't keep trying to explain how. We don't have the time, and however I'm generating this stuff, let's just follow the leads and ask questions later."

After a few moments, Roman reluctantly nodded, but his wavering trust in Drusilla had dipped to almost empty, and he knew Samantha was already there. He would follow her lead, but she would be up front.

"After you," he said nonchalantly, gesturing her past with his hand.

Drusilla looked down at the grating as she crawled past him, but she stopped at Samantha, looked up, her mouth next to her ear, and whispered so he couldn't hear her.

"If you touch him again, I'll kill you."

THIRTY-TWO

Six hours until the planet would come into view. After their extensive crawl through the maintenance tunnels, Samantha had realised where they were actually heading. Not towards the air-free decks they needed to reach, but for an equipment locker in the secondary cargo bay. That was in the opposite direction, and there was only one reason why they would do that. EV Suits. Entering the areas surrounding the bridge would need no more than one of the mobile oxygen units available on every deck in an emergency locker. An EV Suit suggested something else. They were going *outside*.

"Remind me why we're doing this again?" she asked.

"Well, apart from the fact that I figured you'd fancy some fresh air, the doors to the Captain's Quarters were blown away when the bridge breached, which means the only way in is through the emergency escape pod hatch on the outside."

Roman's logic was faultless, but she didn't have to like it. And in truth, she knew that walking along the outside of the ship was far likely to be safer than trying to navigate the inside. EV Suits were great for spacewalks, but they weren't much good in combat. She remembered an ancient sci-fi movie where some human officers fought with a cybernetic organism on the hull of a ship. It didn't end well for one of them, and the other had his suit slashed because he couldn't move quick enough. And she rather doubted she would be dextrous enough to chop off a Raxar's arm and tie it's veins around any holes in her suit.

"Maybe outside isn't a good idea after all," she muttered to herself. She'd tried to tell herself it was safer and then recalled that movie scene and now she was less confident than before.

Drusilla stopped at the exit point for the tunnel they'd been navigating for the last few hours, and held up her hand. Very slowly, she began to open the hatch. She was grateful this was a set of sliding doors rather than a panel. Less chance of dropping it, and just a case of sliding it back if there were monsters outside. Roman and Samantha watched as her head slipped out through the gap. Moments later, her hand gestured for them to move forward. Once they were all out of the hatch, Roman slid it closed. No point telling the enemy where your point of retreat was. Excellent navigation from Drusilla had placed them directly outside the secondary cargo bay. Roman suspected the schematic was buried in her head somewhere, but there wasn't time for indecision. The door to the bay was slightly apart, and a flashing light burst through it intermittently. It was only after Roman widened the gap in the door that he realised it was a hanging light fitting, torn from the ceiling in either the initial asteroid strike, or the engine overload most likely. He didn't want to think it had been dislodged by a crawling Raxar.

Samantha took up position in the doorway, as Drusilla and Roman stalked their way around the inner edge of the room. This cargo bay was less than half the size of the main room, and was usually the place where cargo ships would dock and unload from a circular airlock on the far wall. That airlock in particular was currently being illuminated by an enormous red light, giving it an ominous glow of danger. The equipment locker was located seven metres to the right of the airlock hatch, and once they reached it, Roman signalled Samantha to make her way to their location. So far, so good. No signs of any Raxar. The equipment locker held enough EV Suits and weapons for ten people. On a crew of a thousand, this was deemed the minimum requirement for each room or hatch with a direct route off the ship. When Drusilla opened the hatch, sure enough, there were ten suits and ten disruptor rifles.

One by one, they climbed into the suits. They were typically ostentatious, and exactly what one would expect an establishment attempting to show dominance would wear. The suit itself was a dark blue, with intermittent stripes in thin red lines, going diagonally across the breast. The collar of the suit was emblazoned with five pointed stars. Climbing into the thing felt like encasing Samantha in a red white and blue coffin, with a window. The design of the things was again, as one might expect, driven by the United States. In the late twenty-second century, the tyrant President who was elected by the people, despite the fact he was clearly a stark raving lunatic, declared war. On everyone. The United Kingdom had sided with most of Europe. So much for the 'special relationship.' America, however, partnered with all the cuddliest nations. The United Resistance was formed of the USA, both Koreas, China and Russia. It took nearly ten years, but the rest of the world was defeated. Two years after that, the Deluded In Chief disbanded the United Resistance, and then, one by one, destroyed the nations who had stood by him. All that was left, was America. The irony was, that after all of that, just six weeks later, he died of a heart attack on the lavatory. President Arthur Alexander had wanted to live like a king, and become King of the World. And in the end, he had died like a King. Minus the cheeseburger.

Unfortunately, the garish prominence of the 'star spangled banner' never went away and was adopted by most of the countries as they began to rebuild themselves and regain their own identities, and was eventually adopted by the *Utopia* project marketing departments. They made some excuse about the stars representing Australia, the blue representing multiple European nations, and the red representing the Americas. All nonsense that nobody bought, but everyone went along with.

"What an outfit to die in," Samantha commented as she clipped on the helmet and activated the linked comms inside.

"I don't plan on dying today. I've got a lovely vintage Armani suit still in storage on Azanti Prime and I intend to retrieve it for my burial."

Roman always managed to be more humorous when he delivered a line dead pan. And he knew it. Drusilla simply shook her head, and was already making her way towards the airlock door. Roman called after her.

"Dru? You didn't grab any weapons!"

Of course he knew after he had said it that it had simply been a reflex. As if reading his mind, which of course she was capable of, she gave him his answer.

"You didn't want me armed, so stop pretending."

She turned and started typing in an access code, which again, she should not have known, and Roman and Samantha grabbed more weapons than they probably should have. Each slung a rifle onto the rear harness, and carried another one. As they moved to join Drusilla, Samantha looked down and saw a jagged piece of metal lying on the floor near some other debris.

"Ah what the hell," she said, bending down and sliding it into her belt in the small of her back. "Worked for Worf."

THIRTY-THREE

STANDING ON THE OUTSIDE OF THE ODYSSEY, ROMAN could not help but feel as if he was in a darkened room, shrouded in black curtains, and this was all simply a stage production. The screens had not deceived them. There was nothing. Not a single star in sight. Not even a speck of visible interstellar dust. Until there was.

As the three of them slowly walked along the hull in a vertically diagonal incline, a small amount of light began to shine ahead of them. It was more a reflection than anything else, but it was a pretty good indication that they were approaching a stellar body. The sound made by the gravity boots was triggering Samantha. It sounded like the sort of suction noise you hear when you stepped in something... unpleasant. But after a moment or two, she also noticed the light seemingly coming from nowhere.

Drusilla was the first to reach the top of that hull section. When she stopped, Roman tried to increase his speed to catch up. There it was. Slowly moving closer to them, amongst all of the darkness that surrounded them, was a glowing planet. The world itself was almost pure white. Clouds whisked above the surface, much as they did on Earth, but below the clouds, was nothing but ice. No green land masses, no golden deserts, no sapphire blue oceans. Just ice. And... something else... something *tiny*, but black against the stark glacial surface. It was impossible to tell from this distance what it was, but this was the least of their worries.

The panel on Roman's wrist told them they had only five hours to divert the ship's course, and they weren't even half way to the gaping hole that now sat atop the ship. But the real problem? Directly in their path, lining the hull in front of them, were dozens, no, hundreds. *Thousands* of shimmering black masses attached to the ship. Each one was pulsing slightly, and seemed to be some kind of embryonic sack, and it was fixed to the hull plating with strands of a slick, black, oily vine.

"You've gotta be shittin' me."

Samantha echoed Roman's thoughts perfectly. They weren't safer at all. If anything, they'd just offered themselves up as a newborn's appetisers.

THIRTY-FOUR

I<small>T WAS DIFFICULT TO MAKE OUT, BUT THERE WAS A</small> definite spec in the sky, and it did indeed appear to be moving.

"Nah, no way," said the man to himself, the ice already accumulating in his beard. "No fuckin' way."

He ran back inside the narrow doorway he had come out of, and reached around the corner somewhere, grasping wildly in the dark.

"Where is it? Where the fuck is it?"

He started to shout at himself, blinking away the snow that fell in his eyes. Eventually, he managed to locate what he had been grappling for.

"There she is. You beauty."

The man pulled out a long cylindrical barrelled weapon, similar in design to an old Earth bazooka, only without the rocket. The trigger was in fact a touch pad, and on top of the weapon itself, was a sight. The man took a long look through that sight, gradually increasing the magnification, until his view broke through the atmosphere. He almost dropped the heavy weapon.

213

"The *Odyssey!*" he spoke through a harsh whisper.

His heart hammered and his breath quickened. For a moment he even started to dance on the spot, almost losing his grip on both the weapon and the ice at the same time.

He closed his eyes, took a deep breath full of icy air, and opened his eyes again, slowing his breathing in line with his heartbeat. With a flicker of a smile, he spat the words, "come to Daddy."

The touch pad trigger glowed hot red, and was replaced by an outlined command, with a question mark. The man pressed his forefinger on the button and in response the word 'FIRE' glowed green.

THIRTY-FIVE

THE PATHWAYS BETWEEN THE EGG SACKS WERE NARROW and lined with hazards for a normal sized foot, never mind one encased in a boot three times the size. Drusilla had led the way forward, and almost in response to their presence, the egg sacks had started to glow red, and pulse more violently.

"They know we're here," was all Drusilla said before ploughing through.

Roman stepped exactly where Drusilla had stepped, convinced that whatever was leading her, wanted her unharmed. Samantha, however, was sweating too much with fear, and was now creating condensation inside her suit. She blinked away beads of water, and several steps came incredibly close to triggering one of the vines. She paused for a moment, trying to calm herself, and wishing she could wipe away the moisture inside her helmet. But when she looked back up, Roman and Drusilla were gone.

"Roman? Dru? Can anyone hear me?"

Her panicked words into the microphone went unanswered, and the silence was then punctuated by a warning on her wrist display informing her of a communications failure.

"Fucking wonderful."

One step forward. That was all it took. One step that landed slightly off centre. The attraction of the substance the vines were made of was instant, and Roman felt a pull. Whatever he imagined would happen was nowhere near as bad as the reality. As he yanked his boot free, the vine snapped, and the oily material slid away from his boot like some sort of liquid metal and up onto the now violently pulsing egg sack. He took a couple steps back, making sure not to trip the last two masses before he was in the clear, and watched in awe and absolute terror as one by one, every single egg pouch burst open. A thick black goo erupted from every opening, and drifted away into the emptiness of the void surrounding them. And for a moment, there was nothing. There's no sound in a vacuum, but Roman *heard* the screeches inside his own head. Starting at the back of the nursery, a smaller version of the Raxar leapt out of its cocoon and landed on the hull plating, crouched and primed for attack. It wasn't the eyes now growing in number in front of him that he felt, however, it was to the side of him. As he turned his head and looked through one of the many windows on the exterior of the *Odyssey*, he saw an adult Raxar staring back at him, and smiling. He couldn't explain how, but Roman knew it was the one who had spoken to him. It turned its head slightly in the direction of the younglings, and screeched a battle cry of some sort. Again, Roman heard this in his own head, the telepathic links becoming stronger. He even heard what had been said. The adult had spoken just one word to the offspring.

Feast.

Drusilla had lost communication with Roman and Samantha almost half an hour ago. But she had reached the crater of twisted metal and conduits which previously housed the bridge. Even after almost three weeks in the Expanse, and minimal power, shattered moorings were still sparking. The door to the Captain's Quarters had been torn from its frame, exposing everything inside to the vacuum of space.

"Damn it."

The chances of any evidence or clue as to what was happening to her were likely lost forever. As for the override access console, that would not be easy to get to. Fractured pieces of the *Odyssey's* framework were twisted around the escape pod hatch, the pod itself long torn from the ship. One slight nick from that metal, and Drusilla's EV Suit would be compromised. With no atmosphere inside the room, that would be a huge problem.

"Oh."

She clung to one of the pieces of framework, and glared through the window to the cabin. Two things had caught her attention, and shattered her hopes. The first was the ceiling beam which had fallen straight through the console in question, skewering it like a piece of meat. The second thing was more of an answer to a question. Floating aimlessly in the absence of gravity, was the frozen corpse of Darven.

"Firing mechanism jammed."

The man threw the weapon to the ground in fury. He

ripped a panel off the side, and began rearranging the thin computer modules inside, each one making a small clicking sound as it was first removed, and then replaced. His hands had started to freeze and the snow was getting heavier. He would not be able to survive outside for much longer.

"There!" he screamed triumphantly.

"Firing systems operational."

"Thanks for stating the fucking obvious. Goddamn computers."

Once again, the man hoisted the weapon up onto his shoulder, used the sight to get a new lock on the vessel, and held the touch panel down until it once again turned red, and asked him if he wished to fire.

As he hit the button, and it glowed green once more, a low hum began to form in the chamber of the projectile. It gradually got louder and louder, until the entire barrel was vibrating with the power.

"Boom."

A violent burst of golden light shot up into the sky with such force and heat that it parted the clouds high above. The beam ceased, and the man slumped down onto the ground, his eyes watching as the bolt of energy soared towards its target.

"Down you come."

THIRTY-SIX

Roman had depleted his first power cell and barely made a dent in the armada of creatures surging towards him. He had no idea how long he had been alone, but he was more concerned with staying alive than having no backup. The Raxar offspring were not hurt by the gunfire, but they were knocked off balance and floated away from the ship, which was the next best thing. Roman switched to his rear rifle and began targeting the egg sacks themselves instead. He found shooting one of them free, would take out two or three Raxar in the process. Twice the result for half the power.

At the same time, he was trying to move further and further away, but the Raxar were far faster. And not only were they faster in zero gravity, they were flanking him. One creature leapt onto his back, but lost its grip and floated off, but managed to take his depleted weapon with it. A second leapt in the opposite direction, and its tail whipped across Roman's visor, cracking the glass. A seal integrity warning flashed on his wrist panel, before a third creature leapt onto his active rifle, and snarled in his face. Roman slid the power cell control to maximum and pushed the creature away. As it floated seemingly trying to eat the rifle, confused in its child-like state, Roman smiled to himself. Foolish. He had taken his eye off the ball. Being impaled has a different sensation in space. At first, there is the initial shock that something has happened, followed by an icy burning sensation around the wound site. As Roman slumped to his knees, he looked down, and saw the sharpened end of a juvenile tail sticking out of his side. He could hear the air hissing away into space, and was aware of the red flashing panel on his wrist declaring he was losing oxygen at a rate of twenty percent per minute, but he was also able to *think*. His impending death had seemingly cleared his mind. It was a strange sensation, and he couldn't quite get a handle on it. No, wait. There was another presence there. Who was that? An icy feeling began burning through his mind, and he felt his confusion and panic being forcibly pushed to the side. In his now calmed state, he was able to think coherently. He reached down into his front pocket, and removed the sharpened adult claw from his encounter with the earlier Raxar. With a swift arc, he sliced the edge of the adult tail through the juvenile tail, severing it completely. In it's agony, the juvenile removed the remainder of its tail from Roman's torso, and floated away. Roman grabbed the smaller piece before it moved away, and directed the creature's blood into the hole in his space suit. The feeling was numb. He couldn't feel anything. No emotion, no physical sensations, no effects of decompression. Just clarity. The blood found its way to the wound on his front, and as before, it began to close.

Drusilla stood a few metres behind Roman's now slumped body, her mind channelling everything she had into keeping him calm and stable so that he could work. But the remaining creatures were now heading towards them in a second wave. Drusilla began to feel her hope slipping away, and she gradually started to let Roman go. And then she saw the

Raxar child still clutching the overloading rifle had drifted above the others, and couldn't help but smirk.

The explosion was quite something. The first Raxar was incinerated. There would be no regenerating from that, of which Drusilla was certain. The resulting shockwave not only burned through several hundred of the creatures below, but blew a second crater in the ship. The scene was quite something to behold. There was the initial explosion, followed by the remaining offspring falling into the newly formed hole in the ship, before the decompression effect took hold, and sucked them all back out and into space, even taking a few of the adults with them.

Drusilla clambered down from her position and started moving towards Roman. He couldn't have more than a minute or so left of air, and was already unclipping her reserve transfer hose from her belt. She saw in the distance, that Samantha was coming into view, and when she saw Roman slumped on the deck and the visible air leakage, she disengaged her gravity boots, and kicked off from the hull. She set her sights on Roman and kept them locked there as she powered forward on momentum alone. She grabbed a nearby dislodged piece of ship's framework, and lowered herself back down to the hull, continuing to move towards him. He was hurt. No, not like this. She'd save him.

But she didn't get the chance.

In the blink of an eye, a bright golden flash pierced the darkness, and blinded them all momentarily. It hit the underside of the *Odyssey* with such force, it blew a hole clean through the ship, and out the other side. The *Odyssey* went into a spin, knocked off from its flight path, it caught the edge of the planet's gravity and began to be drawn in. The force of the explosion had sent Samantha cartwheeling backwards, and down into the newly created hole, falling into a random section of the ship. The violent spinning increased, and Drusilla could feel the suit heating up as they came towards the outer atmosphere. They wouldn't survive this. Their only hope was to get inside the ship. She staggered forward and grabbed a hold of Roman's arms. She deactivated his gravity boots to make it easier to move him, and dragged him as quickly as she could to the crater his weapon had just blown in the ship. She reactivated his boots and pushed his helmet downwards, and he floated into the ship's structure, the confirming sound a second or two later of his boots magnetising to a floor somewhere.

Drusilla smiled at the conformation he was inside, but then the ship rocked violently in the opposite direction, as a piece of the nose broke away, and spiralled toward her. There was no time to move. No time to think. She closed her eyes as the piece of the ship skewered her body in place, crushing her ribs, and vital organs into the hull below, leaving only her head exposed. By some miracle, the air supply was still flowing, and as her blood began to flow out of her mouth, she saw the icy surface of the planet coming into view.

"What a beautiful place," she thought.

EPILOGUE

THE ROOM WAS BRIGHT. THE LIGHTS HERE WERE OF AN incredible volume, and the sudden switch from darkness to such illumination was agonising. Instruments crashed and rattled to the floor, as her limbs tried to block it from her eyes.

"Hey, hey, wait a minute, calm down, it's okay!"

The voice was warm and comforting, but she still could not see. In response, the man walked over to the wall, and dimmed the lights in the room to a more bearable level.

"Sorry about that, with the surface so bright, I find it easier to keep my eyes adjusted to that level, then the blindness is... less."

She coughed and spluttered, blood spraying from her mouth and onto the floor. Opening her eyes once more, she was able to adjust much more easily.

"Where, where am I?" she asked, her voice strangled and raspy.

"You're in my medical room. You were dead when I brought you in here. Should've known you wouldn't let death stop you."

Confusion was just one sensation going through her body.

The feeling that she was... incomplete. Missing something. She felt her heart rate increasing, and in turn a nearby machine beeped furiously.

"No, no, calm down. I brought you back once, but I don't think we should chance it a second time, Dru."

Drusilla's eyes snapped open at the sound of her name, and she bolted upright, unaware that she had only been covered by a thin modesty sheet. She leapt off the table and immediately, her legs gave way and she crumpled into a heap. Now shivering, cold, naked and terrified, she grabbed both sides of her head and started pulling at her hair.

"Drusilla, stop. Look at me."

She resisted, but the man kept trying to persuade her, and after a moment or two, he managed to get her to stand up, using him as a crutch, and he led her back to the table, before draping a nearby coat over her shoulders.

"Are you okay?" he asked.

She nodded.

And then she looked at him. Impossible. The images before that she had been bombarded with were impossible, but this was *impossible*.

The face was older, certainly. More wrinkles, the long and scraggly beard covering much of the lower half of his face, and his hair now shoulder length. But that smile was there. She'd seen it in photographs. She'd seen the worry carved into it in his warning message back at the start of this nightmare.

Standing in front of Drusilla, over a hundred and fifty years since he recorded that message, was Admiral Harry Ransome.

"So, you do still remember me then?"

ACKNOWLEDGMENTS

I have to thank several people for this one. When I first decided I was going to leave the Dark Corner Series behind, I was a little reticent, but I wanted to begin paving the way for what would come next. I had enjoyed writing *Resurrection* despite it not being my finest work, and I had loved the raw violence and gore of *Frame of Mind*. And then I read a book by S.A. Barnes, which combined the two. The book was called *Dead Silence* and was a sci-fi horror that I absolutely devoured. Terrifying, gripping, and the perfect blend of sci-fi and horror. I wanted to do that. And I didn't want to wait. So I must thank S.A. Barnes for that because they inspired me to make the decision to begin this story.

I must also thank Christian Francis, for a variety of things. For formatting this book for me, designing the original cover, and donating yet more of his resources allowing me to take the book wide. I have come to truly relish my friendship with him and I hope he knows what an impact he has made on me as a writer. Particularly with his novelisation of the 1985 movie *Titan Find*. The gore in that story inspired me to continue writing *Horizon* even when I thought it was never going to be finished. In fact, I'm typing this just 20 hours before the submission deadline. It is the closest I have ever come to missing one. I'd also like to thank him for taking Horizon under the *Echo On* name. It gives you a newfound faith in yourself, when somebody else is willing to put their name on your books. Gives you a huge incentive to not make them shit.

I thank my wife, Charlotte, for sticking by my and encouraging me to go off into the office and write even when she had been at work all day, and for desperately harping on at me to send her the first half of the book so she could proofread it and correct it for me whilst I worked on the second half. She is solely responsible for the description of one of the more gruesome deaths in the story having offered to rewrite my version with a little more... let's say pizzazz. She is always my rock.

Writing this book started as a pure unbridled passion project, but it was struck with several setbacks. Moving 100 miles away to a new home in Dorset, meant I lost over a month of time to work on this story. I hit a writers block FOUR TIMES writing this one, the most I've ever had with any book. And then of course I started dictating where the story was going by envisaging what came next. Never do that.

A wise man once said on a clock-themed app, finish the plot, not the story. So that's what I did. I hope. There is absolutely no need for me to write a sequel to Horizon at all. I left intrigue at the end, almost a cliffhanger of sorts. But I don't necessarily have to resolve it. I could just let you all go mad...

...but you know me too well by now.

ABOUT THE AUTHOR

David was born in 1988 in Wolverhampton, England. He spent most of his youth growing up in nearby Telford, where he attended the prestigious Thomas Telford School. However, unsure of which direction he wished his life to go in, he left higher education during sixth form, in order to get a job and pay his way. He has spent most of his life since, working in retail.

In 2007, following the death of his grandfather William Henry Griffiths a couple of years earlier, David's family relocated to the North Devon coastal town of Ilfracombe, where he got a job in local greengrocers, Normans Fruit & Veg as a general assistant, and spent 8 happy years there. In 2014, David met Charlotte, and in 2016, relocated to Plymouth to live with her as she continued her University studies.

In 2018, the pair were married, and currently reside on the Isle of Portland, Dorset.

The first published works of David's, was *The Dark Corner*. It was a compilation of short haunting stories which he wrote to help him escape the reality of the Coronavirus pandemic in early-mid 2020. However, it was not until January 2021, that he made the decision to publish.

From there, all literary hell broke loose...

tiktok.com/@davidwadams.author

amazon.com/stores/author/B08VHD911S

Made in the USA
Columbia, SC
12 June 2024

37050652R00135